Cars

George
Bowering

Ryan
Knighton

Cars

Coach House Books

first edition

Published with the assistance of the Canada Council for the Arts and the Ontario Arts Council

NATIONAL LIBRARY OF CANADA CATALOGUING IN PUBLICATION DATA

Bowering, George, 1935-
    Cars / George Bowering, Ryan Knighton.

ISBN 1-55245-115-1

    I. Knighton, Ryan II. Title.

PS8503.O875C27 2002   C813'.54   C2002-904104-X
PR9199.3.B63C37 2002

The beauty of men never disappears
But drives a blue car through the stars.

*M*y father was idling at a red light once, then decided it was a good time to go ahead and light his smoke. In those days both my parents were loyal to minty cigarettes so foul and distasteful I won't name them. They got me started, though, those cool smokes. As a kid they resembled dessert, the cigarettes, but that's probably because Ma froze all the smokes in empty Lighthouse salad dressing jars, the glass ones. Our house always had a fridge freezer stacked with jars of fresh cigarettes next to the ice cream and Eggos. And that's how I started. They looked tasty, all white and frozen and minty fresh. That summer, my first job was stuffing flyers for the *Langley Advance*. I felt ahead of my time, the only fourteen-year-old I knew who worked graveyard shifts. Pretty cool, eh? Dad had worked graveyards, too, so it seemed logical I likewise take up smoking. I was going to be just like him before anybody else. Every day I'd smuggle three cigarettes in an empty Billy Idol cassette case – one for each break. Work was next to King Tut's Tavern, so you could anticipate gassed-up plumbers harassing you for free morning papers around 2 AM. They could act pretty strange, but I didn't let it startle me. I'd stand there giving them an Easter Island stone face, coolly smoking my minty smoke, just like my dad would have. Anyway, the light is still red and he's still idling. His dashboard lighter pops out ready to go. He casually presses the gas, starting through the intersection, thinking he's just heard it go green. I've listened many times, but I've never heard a traffic light change colour. Apparently it sounds something like an anticipated cigarette lighter.

In the winter of 1955 a bunch of us were driving west on Highway 2 in a 1951 Monarch and boy was it cold. That's the one that went in the ditch in Minnesota, but I'll be telling that story another time. When we stopped for gas in Fargo the young gas jockey looked hard at the hood ornament and the name in chrome. They didn't have Monarchs in the USA, and he thought it was a customized Mercury. In the fifties young guys like us were always customizing their cars. I think he wanted to buy this car. In the summer of 1956, my roommate Fred Bing and I were driving west on Highway 2 in his 1954 Meteor, and when we stopped for gas in Fargo this gas guy didn't know what to make of it, because they didn't have Meteors in the USA either. Those USAmericans don't know about anything if it isn't from the USA. He thought it was a customized Ford, I think. I don't remember whether it was the same gas guy, probably not. Now I have just recently been reading *Mauve Desert* by Nicole Brossard. In *Mauve Desert* the teenage girl is always driving her mother's old Meteor into the desert. Now I don't know whether Nicole Brossard knows that the USAmericans didn't have Meteors. Maybe she just liked the name. If the novel took place in Anglo Ontario instead of Arizona, maybe that girl would have driven a Monarch.

A firetruck reversed into my mother's car once and screwed it all up. The transmission was fucked, the engine was gibbled, the nose and grill were crumpled – it was a mess. We're going back a ways before I was around. Ma was a short woman in a small sports car. She went to work each morning, a psychiatric nurse in a convertible Triumph so low to the ground you could reach out and touch the pavement from inside. From inside the car, that is. At any rate, the settlement went ahead without a hitch. Those kind taxpayers in Maple Ridge unknowingly agreed to pay for whatever the parts and labour. Now enter Ma's brothers. These two coaxed the mechanic to throw in some unnecessary custom work on their tab. Thrown in on the taxpayers' tab, that is. They – her goofy brothers – reasoned it would be some fun if their mechanic buddy crossed the car's overdrive to Ma's reverse gear. The story ends with the brothers picking her up at work outside Riverview Psychiatric Hospital to deliver her Triumph. What else could have happened but they scared her stupid driving ahead in reverse away from the so-called loony bin.

*A*s the mercury climbs in the South Okanagan these days, such as August 11, 2001, people are awfully glad they can take their air conditioning for granted, though of course I haven't had air conditioning in my 1990 Volvo for three summers. What does it matter? In 1959 there wasn't any air conditioning in the South Okanagan, but there were Fahrenheit degrees, lots of them. What you wished for was a convertible, and while you were at it, why not a Cadillac convertible? My buddy Willy would say to a girl from Osoyoos, maybe, 'Want to go for a spin in my snappy red convertible?' and what he had was a 1954 Morris Minor with the top sawed off. This was the best joke going in the South Okanagan that summer, and to tell the truth, I was envious. A year later his stepfather had some more sawing done – well, he used to have a machine shop – and it became the smallest pickup truck in that part of the valley, and Willy used it for everything. Imagine, sitting in a red Morris Minor pickup truck, ogling girls we knew.

*W*hen it comes to taxis we all know you're as phony as a wicker pisspot if you say you can go without watching the meter and its growing demands. This is for many our most common experience of the old challenge not to think of a pink polar bear for the next thirty seconds.

Insert pink polar bear here:_____.

Essentially, taxis are an uncomfortable hybrid of the car and that infernal clock. Measure your passage, that's what they do. But any ride starts at about two dollars and fifty cents. What I want to know is how we missed all that go by. As our Ethel Wilson writes, just once I would like the driver to stop the clock for ten cents' worth of view. But that's not their business, the taxis. It's not even the job of a pink polar bear.

Insert view here:_____.

In the central Okanagan Valley we lived not that far from the lake, in Peachland – all the names in that part of the country were like that. For instance, the next town over was Summerland. What year was it exactly, maybe 1939, but of course this was a little before I took heed of years and their numbers. One time down at the lake, where the clear water waved over pebbles in the sunlight, my father was showing me how to skip stones. Here were some numbers worth learning, and now for the first time in my life I realize that he was teaching me to count. He skipped his best one eleven times, long flight of stone, eastward. It went halfway across Lake Okanagan. Go and have a look. Another time I was standing alone in our front yard where the little leafy arch was over the front gate and that always seemed to come into one's memory along with the song 'Stardust' and watching a Model A Ford, black or dark green like them all, rolling by eastward with no one in it, rolling with moderate speed down toward the lake. The Model A Ford had the nicest shape ever given to an automobile.

I have heard it quoted on several occasions that the poet George Stanley is rumoured to drive the wind. Or maybe it's 'like the wind.'

One hot summer day in 1958 I boiled fish in the radiator of a little square Land Rover. We were having the worst forest-fire season in history, and all the Forest Service vehicles were busy, so we rented whatever we could get. I got the smallest Land Rover going, cute little jeep thing. It was painted bright yellow and had McCulloch chainsaw pictures all over it. So, as I drove the logging roads of the Merritt forest district, I belted out the McCulloch Chainsaw song:

> You're in luck when you've got a McCulloch Chainsaw
> You've got power by the hour in your hand
> With McCulloch you're the master
> 'Cause you keep on cuttin' faster
> You're in luck when you've got a McCulloch Chainsaw

My job for the while was driving groceries up to a firefighting camp and picking up their order for the next day. Sometimes when you are driving up a dirt logging road you meet a loaded million-tonne logging truck on its terrifying way down, and you learn how to jam the gearshift and drive in reverse very fast down the twisting mountainside road until you find a place to get off the road without going off a cliff. Well, the fish. After a while the radiator sprung a leak and I had to carry several pails of water along with the groceries. At the camp I filled the pails with water dipped from the lake. You know the rest. Partway down the hill I opened the hot hot ouch radiator and looked inside, and there they were, floating. I don't remember whether they were still there when we returned the little yellow Land Rover to the chain-saw dealer.

*I*n his superfantastic autobiography William Carlos Williams taunted us wannabe poets with God's hand. He proposed that the one thing God can't do is raise and lower her hand at the same time. Only art tries her luck at this, he manoeuvred. I don't know about that, but if you look at your driver's feet you'll see why I think this is true of smoke shows. In a Langley Esso station, the gas-pump oasis where my high school buddy Jason worked in a backwards baseball cap, I learned how to burn rubber the Williams way. Jason showed me in his parents' VW Rabbit how to lay into the contradictory brake and gas pedals at the same time. If you could get it just right, your dad's station wagon could produce a wicked cloud of blue smoke behind you. I tried it on my dad's Acadian but only succeeded in jerking the car over a speed bump and dislodging the stupid muffler. Later I blamed the chugging noises on a sharp speed bump in the McDonald's drive-thru. Brand names always seemed to lend credibility to such stories. Now I suspect the other thing God can't do is drive a Model A Ford around BC's interior without a soul steadying the wheel.

*T*hose were the days when all the poets attended pub night at the Cecil, and we lived, Angela and I and baby Thea, with George Stanley, at 2249 York Avenue in Kitsilano. It was not a long way from the Cecil to York Avenue, and the sixties were not quite over in 1971, but there were some Vancouver aldermen with long sideburns. Because it was not all that far from the Cecil to York Avenue, we went there and back in my maroon 1965 Chevrolet Bel Air, which I had driven from Montreal with two chihuahuas. George Stanley took his chances. He is an unpretentious scholarly man who likes to go to the bar, in this case the Cecil Pub, which was really a beer parlour in the old western Canadian sense, terry cloth, even, elasticized around the tops of the round tables. We poets went to the Cecil around 10 PM, after the college boys had got lucky or drunk and gone home or elsewhere. When the pub closed, if we were not going to the Arts Club or the Luv-A-Fair, we would drive home, or I would, over the Burrard Street bridge, and now George Stanley was pretty drunk but his tie was still not loosened much, and he took his chances. I would pretend to be drunk but I really was drunk, and trying to disconcert George Stanley I would boast in a loud voice, 'I can drive like the wind!' That usually did the trick. Sometimes I said, 'I can drive when I can't walk!' Sometimes, if I felt that the occasion required it, I would announce, 'I know where every fender is on this car!' I had learned that one from my old buddy Willy Trump, who could not drive a car any more because he was blind even when he was sober.

*T*axis and their clocks. I was putting in my time at the college where I teach. The office was dead so I checked my home voice mail to see if anyone wanted to talk to me from somewhere else. Three peculiarly alarming messages from my father were waiting, all back to back. Flat tone, very curt. Call me. Ryan. Ryan, call me. Call me. I did. My brother had just died. My parents were in the hospital with my other brother and my sister and some close family friends. I said I'd be there as fast as I could be there, but part of me (do we really have parts? some spare?) carried on as if nothing was happening. How would I get to Langley from North Vancouver, this part of me wondered. I don't drive. I could take a taxi but that would cost about sixty bucks. I don't have sixty bucks right now. I can't go. Someone will have to come and get me if I'm going to go. It's an interesting defence. I don't have enough money for this to be real. Try again later. Thanks for calling. I took a cab, of course, and for the first time I didn't watch the meter. Honest, I didn't. Then, two years later, I took a cab from my house to the college in North Vancouver where I still teach. The bus strike forced me to do this more often than I cared to afford, but I didn't think much about that. I'd always rather take a cab if I can get away with it. They're so much faster than public transit, taxis and their clocks. And there are so many fewer people to negotiate. The cab driver swung us around to McGill and headed for the Ironworkers Memorial Bridge. A man is rumoured to be petrified in one of the bridge's concrete pillars after that famous collapse. The cabbie said, I remember you, I've driven you before. Not an uncommon remark, I thought, a blind, bald and tattooed college teacher like myself running about as common in this town as a blind, bald and tattooed dodo breeder. Cab drivers who recognize me seem to abound, though. I drove you to a hospital in Langley, he said. There was something wrong with your, your, brother. He was sick or something. Is he feeling any better? Two years later and I wasn't caught up enough to answer his question. Pretty spooky. Now, I don't mean to confuse the issue. Taxi doesn't mean what metaphor means, but they both carry something across for you. It's in them to do that. Both go across bridges with you, petrified by time.

*O*ne day a few years ago I was driving north just about at the north end of Vaseux Lake. And nearly hit a beautiful deer that was bouncing across the road in front of my car. It was the spot where my mother got hit by the flying cow. There was a dent in the front of our light green 1947 Plymouth, and my mother said a cow came flying into the front of the car. They don't fly, cows, she was informed. It must have been hit by a car coming in the opposite direction, was her conclusion. Mostly, over all these years, we have believed her, about that and other things. But one dark night we were getting ready to go home after a night of badminton at the high school gym, my mother and I. This is how we got a dent in the back of the Plymouth. My mother backed up confidently into the rear corner of a pickup, and there was a kind of car-thunk sound. 'Who put that thing there?' asked my mother. I use that line sometimes now. Once I heard my father say it when he stubbed his toe on a railroad track.

*N*ot long after Allen Ginsberg died, Stan Persky organized an immense reading and memorial by various local poets. Pub Night II was adjourned for the occasion. Because the Western Front was packed with listeners, there were many breaks and many beers to fill the breaks. I remember Gerry Gilbert read a poem with the line 'where there's fries, there's the *Province*.' At night's end, four of us finally squeezed ourselves and my hiccups into a cab. We had just turned east on Broadway when the cabbie looked at me in his rear-view and shouted, Hey, I recognize you! From hiccup where? I asked. You were in my cab last week! Uh, hiccup no, I don't think hiccup so. You must have me hiccup mistaken for somebody else. Hiccup. He turned around in his seat at the next red light and looked at me hard. Yeah, it was you, I recognize you! You stiffed me for twenty bucks! You gimme my money now! No I hiccup didn't! Yes you did! No hiccup I didhiccupn't! It went on like this for eight blocks. I thought this taxi driver was going to clean my clock. Always taxis and their clocks. Let's just calm down, I said. He was a big bearded man with a Buddha belly wedged under the steering wheel. In cartoons you're supposed to rub an angry person's belly to soothe them, but I thought better of it. Are you sure, I asked, you had a blind, bald and tattooed man in your car last week? Why the hell do you think it was me who stiffed you? No answer, then a polite, How are your hiccups, sir? Huh? How are your hiccups? Uh, gone maybe, but why do you … He slapped his hands on the steering wheel and laughed. I scared 'em out of you, didn't I! I knew I could scare 'em out of you! Wits, I'm telling you, I haunt a town of wits looking for a fix.

*I*t's a lot easier to get a taxi in Montreal than it is in Vancouver. It is also easier to run into one with your car. I once ran into one with my car Arnold, the 1965 maroon two-door Bel Air. In my defence I have to say that I was driving north, or as the Montrealers say, east, on Ste-Catherine Street at night, with a car full of family and rowdies – well, not really rowdies, but people who were talking loudly and non-stop, or at least my dear wife Angela and I think our friend Stan or maybe Tony, and there were in those days many many bright and colourful lights along Ste-Catherine Street. So, at the corner of Bishop Street, how was I supposed to pick out the red traffic light among all the other red and green lights (and I failed that test in the RCAF anyway) telling us about barbecued chicken places and so on? Well, a taxi was going through the intersection, but everyone was talking at once and the windows were steamed up and no one was telling me about the red traffic light, so I sort of hit the taxi on its starboard side with the very front of my Bel Air. If I remember rightly, I didn't receive much in the way of damage to the front of my fine GM product. But there was a pretty good dent in the door of the cab. Well, you know what happens, you pull over somewhere into an illegal parking spot, but that's okay under the circumstances, and you yank out your wallet. But I was surprised to find that I was not carrying my wallet. This is the beginning of the amazing part – the taxi driver drove me all the way home to Grosvenor Avenue to get my wallet to show him my licence and insurance card, and then when I found out that there was no cash in the wallet to pay the taxi fare, he let me write him a cheque, and how was he to know that I would have to postdate the cheque because it was a little while till payday. And then he drove me back uptown for free. What, I said to my passengers when I got back to my unheated car and there was no parking ticket, but if there had been, would this taxi driver offer to pay it, a nice man, that cabbie, who was not going to be able to drive his car professionally until he had the dent fixed. So now when I take a cab in Montreal, I always tip big, even when the cabbie is a newly arrived Haitian who is not really familiar with the location of the place I want to get to.

In those days we had Pub Night II: The Sequel. The authentic Pub Night had long vacated the Cecil. Its owners had grown weary with the artsy-fartsy crowd so they tried to scare everyone away with serious country and western music. It didn't work, but the strippers later trimmed the numbers back, mostly because it was unfair to our buddy Blind Willy. So, twenty years later, Pub Night II officially moved to Shenanigans between the voulez-vous dancefloor and Vancouver's finest ESL students. Playing cards were stuck willy-nilly to the ceiling for some reason. If you came super-early you'd know Blind Willy was always there first, Blind Willy Trump with his two glasses of beer at a time. Don't ask me why. I've heard it has something to do with the physics of keeping beer cold. If you're lucky, you might receive one of Willy's informative Spanish braille lessons with your nacho chips as flashcards. Ah, Trumped again! The first night I joined the Pub Night II rabble, George and I excused ourselves at the same time in order to catch our respective buses home. We walked down to Hastings Street together and every time I bumped into a pole or tripped on a curb he teased me about my suave but evidently useless white-cane style. Together we waited in the cold at the bus stop with our hands jammed deep into our respective pockets. A bus approached and George squinted as he tried to read the number. It grew bigger and approached faster, but still George couldn't read the number. Is it a #14 or a #22? C'mon #22! he hooted. But the bus didn't bother to let him get a good look or let him get on, it just sailed by. In my mind I like to picture some warm people inside waving for good measure. I'm a pal, though, so as the bus whizzed past us I stuck out my white cane and dragged it like a finger along a bit of the side. Feels like a #22, I confirmed. Most Pub Nights since then George bugs me to explain how exactly that works.

Some of my cars I named and some I didn't. Some of the names I can remember and some I can't. Our cream and red 1954 Austin was named Brünhilde. We always agreed on the names, Angela and I. Our maroon 1965 Chevy Bel Air was Arnold. That is just what he was. I think I once had a car with the name Victor. Later, when we both had cars, I had a Honda named Jane. By that time I was buying those Japanese cars and I can't remember what years they were. When you are a kid, so everyone says, you know all the cars. If you're a boy. Now all the cars look alike, and they have silly brand names. Elantra or something. When I was a kid my mother said all the cars looked alike to her. Anyway, after our two-tone green 1954 Bel Air took us through all the dangers of Mexico, we were discussing what name to give it at last. Believe I'll call him Saviour, I said, and right away Angela agreed.

*O*ften I hitch a lift to Capilano College with my pal Sharon Thesen because we both live in East Vancouver. Our trek takes us over the Ironworkers Memorial Bridge to what we affectionately call The Plant or The Crap, depending. Her car often occurs in our shared morning imagination as a kind of free-wheeling confessional or post-Jungian transportable couch. On our minds you'll more often than not find poetry in the way other people might spend rush hour haunted by their developmental chains of childhood. Memory leaps from the back seat and *Boo!* But poetry, as we commiserate with exaggeration, has abandoned us in the woods with only crumbs. Lots of verse, little poetry. The American poet Lou Welch tells the story of how he was part of a sleepy museum tour group once and how the tour guide was intoning her laconic and monotonous speech for the forty-eighth time that day when a shaggy dog bolted through the stuffy room and between the stage-weary tour guide and her dozing crowd. The spell was broken for a second by this dog's capacity to introduce each person to the others' consciousnesses. What the hell was that? Where'd it come from? Where'd it go? Yabber yabber yabber, continued the crowd and the tour guide. Welch says a poem should do that, too. It should act like that dog. Of course Sharon agrees and looks for a parking spot in the tidy arrangement of a vast and indistinguishable lot. Some mornings you can hear hundreds of dogs in their pens because there's a dog kennel just behind the college. The noise breaks the sterility of our lot. Sometimes, after night classes, when nobody's around, Creative Writing instructors howl at the North Vancouver moon. Really. Scout's honour.

*M*y girlfriend Joan's girlfriend is turning twenty-one, a young dewy lady in the acting profession, and we have a night ahead of us. When I was with Joan I experienced a lot of first times, though she was my second, and come to think of it, Ryan, that would make for another interesting book to collaborate on. Some of the first times were the first time I ever went to a nightclub, the first time I ever had a half a peach in a glass of champagne for breakfast, and the first time I ever saw Corinna's breast. So Corinna's date for the night is Ian Thorne, an English guy, pretty short, actor, somewhat older than the rest of us. I think I remember that Ian borrowed some money off Joan for this great twenty-first birthday, but Ian Thorne liked eccentric extravagance. So the car we were in was a wood-panelled Bentley, and I think the engine was made by Hawker-Siddeley, which was an English airplane engine maker I remembered from the air force. Anyway, we were on crowded Granville Street going north, in the days when it was the main drag, neon flushing the sky. Ian had to run in and buy something, so he told me to drive around the block a couple times because there were zero parking spots. This huge car with huge headlights, and what if I hit something, and did I have a driver's licence? Ian did not know that I had very little driving experience and none of it while drinking and most of it on tractors. But he liked a kind of bravado nonchalance, should have been wearing an English turn-of-the-century cape. So I slid over, and this glamorous car had its own snobbish England way of doing things. The gearshift, I remember, was a stick that came out to the right off the steering column, and you didn't so much move the stick as you moved something along or around the stick. Well, I couldn't really figure it out, and I had two beautiful lively young women in the car, and a lot of colourful noisy traffic outside, so I found one gear and just stayed in it as I made about eight right turns, signalling with my arm out the window. This was about 1960 or 1961, I think. I was a lot taller than Ian Thorne, but I was glad to hand over the wood-panelled Bentley, or maybe the car was a Hawker-Siddeley.

*A*s I say, often I hitch a lift with Sharon to The Plant. It's encouraging how I read Sharon's wonderful poem 'I drive the car' five years ago and now – whaddaya know? – she does! Poetry is still an honest Joe. Last year, Sharon picked me up in a shapely silver Audi. Very beautiful. It makes a terrific sound when it goes, and it does. About three years back I read a poem of hers in which 'silver imports sleep that bad, bad night away – oh yes they do'. And they do! Sharon doesn't seem to welch on any promises in her poems. As I say, she introduced me to the work of Lou Welch and his startling dog, so there's no mystery. The day Sharon picked me up in her silver import she had to run a couple errands before work. On the way we talked about *Ronin*, that stylish Euro-thriller with Jean Reno and Robert De Niro, a film littered with tripped-out Audis screaming through the cobblestoned streets of Nice. Check it out. Rows of cars, all identical, peeling past sidewalk cafes and startled *flâneurs*. We parked in front of this little office in an industrial park and whaddaya know but she opened her door and an alarming alarm peeled from every corner of the car. Sharon frantically pressed buttons on her computerized fob and toggled switches and depressed buttons all over the dash. Nothing. We got out of the car and shut the doors. Nothing. The little industrial office workers clapped their windows shut and pulled the blinds. It continued. Then Sharon, always in control, smartly took the Audi manual from the glove box, a glossy tome with an index roughly as thick as my first book of poems. She looked up A for Alarm. Nothing relevant. She looked up S for Security. Nothing. Desperate, she looked up N for Noise. Zip. The alarm went on. To make a long noise short, soon a button was found and we drove away, the little street of office fronts shut up tight as a ghost town. I was startled to learn from Sharon that Welch, besides being a poet of note, is primarily known for being the author of that famous bug-killing slogan. You know the one: Raid – Kills Bugs Dead. It is said Welch wandered off into the forest one day and was never heard from again. Maybe it was the advertising business that got him, maybe it was poetry, or maybe it was the speed between the two. Once he wrote a poem about walking off into the woods, and later he did just that. All I can say is I hope he took with him the hammer that killed John Henry.

*I*f you are going to have a head-on collision, Ryan, have it at as low a speed as possible under the circumstances – that's my advice. This was how my red 1972 Datsun came to an end. It was the first new car I ever bought – $2,500, with money from a novel I optioned to a filmmaker who never did. So here I was, at or really nearly at my familiar drive from Vancouver to Oliver, to see my mum in the late seventies, I guess. This would be at her new place, up the hill a little from Oliver's little old airstrip. I was on the only straight stretch on Highway 97, getting ready to turn right, when a car coming south turned into my lane, no signal or anything, you know that nightmare. I stepped on the brake as hard as I could, thanking some being or luck that I was alone, my wife and daughter back in Van. Well, he didn't seem to share my attitude toward braking, and if I went left I'd be in a worse head-on, and to the right was a deep ditch and probably this guy still coming. Well, I can tell you, the sound of a collision is hateful. But there we were. The inside of a 1972 Datsun is not commodious, and I banged my forehead against the metal strip at the top edge of the windshield. The guy in the other car is also alive, and glory be, he was to blame a hundred percent. He was a thin guy in his eighties. I thought there was a side road there, he said. Well, I said, there isn't, and even if there was, you are required to wait until I am gone before you turn left across the highway. Now it turns out that he has no driver's licence because he did this kind of thing too often and had it taken away from him. Even better – he turns out to be a retired dentist who years before had led a campaign against me and my *Oliver Chronicle* column because I was a Communist agent and he was the local leader of Ron Gostick's Canadian Intelligence Service, a religious Cold War outfit that warned against communists, atheists, Jews, homosexuals, feminists, intellectuals and hippies. Boy! The insurance people gave me about $2,000 for my car, but now it was years later and any little Japanese car would cost about $10,000. However, the only really sad part was that the radio in my Datsun was famous for its ability to pull in radio stations from halfway across the continent. My brother and my friends Dwight and Paul said I should have gone to the wrecking yard in OK Falls and snagged that radio.

*O*nce I drove through SurDel with Michael Turner to take pictures of monster houses and not-so-monster houses. The houses would speak for themselves in his oral narrative, 'SurDel', which I would later publish as a real-estate flyer in a respectable literary mag. How better to present the story of a suburban development project like the SurDel border? I remember it as a great drive and a good piece. Don't remember when this was exactly, but I recall we passed the Cariboo exit on the Trans-Canada when we agreed the experimental sixties of Canadian novels had seriously detoured in 1988 with *In the Skin of a Lion*. Or maybe we should just say something stalled for the most part and leave it at that. We're still there, we agreed, still there writing that book over and over, some of us are. Not far from the number 10 highway, some of the monster houses are large and crowded enough in their culs-de-sac that you can't stand across the street and fit a single one comfortably inside the camera's frame. The understated older house we photographed that day from the car was much more interesting to look at, anyway. It actually had character, which was what it would have to stand for in Michael's piece. The monster houses don't really have character because character is a particular matter of presence, the kind you can measure with the quivering property values next door. This older house with character was a boxy seventies rancher with a broken-down El Camino wedged in the driveway, and the house featured an ugly but impressive pile of dirt dumped right square in front of the living room picture window. Okay, I know what you're thinking. This is supposed to be the moment in the story when I'm supposed to wish I had told Michael something, something deep and deeply felt that day as we drove home along the Trans-Canada. Nine famous Canadian novelists might say they – wait for it – longed, that they longed to tell him something that day as they drove home. People are always longing in cars, even on the Trans-Canada. But that's the problem, right? The novel is always long and your neighbour is zoned to live only a few yards away from you. So maybe you should just open the window like this: 'Hey, Michael! While you're here, do you think the real subject of sadness was buried under that pile of sentiment some people keep on diggin'?'

One thing I can tell you for sure is that George Stanley does not or did not drive like the wind. He drove like an unmarried older lady going to the Safeway parking lot. I hope he doesn't mind my saying so. Well, he once got his revenge for all those nights whizzing home from Pub Night at the Cecil. He was a teacher of some sort, an English teacher plus whatever else those community colleges get a person to do, up north, mainly Terrace, where my dad went amazingly by car for his first teaching job, but maybe I will get to that story another time. A lot of my car stories are dad stories, of course. And in the Sequel to Pub Night there were tads and dads, and that is yet another story. Now, George Stanley's revenge. The only place I know of where George Stanley ever had a car was up there in Terrace, and if he had to go teach in Stuart he would go by plane if it wasn't socked in, but closer campuses he could reach by car. I was up there for a number of poetry readings or prose readings, and George was my host; that is the kind of wonderful thing that used to happen when there were poets at all the community colleges in the province. George was in charge of my getting to other places, one of those places that start with K, and at least one of the Hazeltons. So he has a not by any means new or even all that recent big USAmerican-type car, like most other people up there in that time, those who did not have a pickup truck with a toolbox, a broom and a German shepherd in the back. Out on the road he took me, and I am wondering: when did George learn to drive, or do you really have to learn up here? And I swear. He is looking out the windshield along that long hood all right, but he is looking from lower than the arc of the top of the steering wheel, if you know what I mean. Heh heh, he says in that wonderful humorous George Stanley voice you have to have heard to know what I mean, I can drive like the wind, and he followed that with a string of exclamation points. He had been waiting years to say this. I quaked in my passenger seat but I did not pee my pants. Boy, it was wonderful in those days. I even looked out at the Skeena River from time to time.

*A*s I say, people are always longing in cars, and they long in Penticton, too. Six years ago, my buddy Peter and I were camping just outside the town and made a stupid judgment in the order of things. If you ever go camping, don't drink the Silent Sam before you set up the campsite. The sun was laying black rubber over the lake so we decided to hoof it into town and try to happen upon a nightclub or a pub for something less practical but equally boozy to do. Away we meandered in cut-offs down the late-night road, only to discover we were a hefty hike farther from town than we'd imagined, so we decided to hitch. About ten minutes later, the loudest car I've ever heard picked us up. People are always longing out loud in cars. Remember, it's dark out and I can't see too hot to begin with. That's why Peter is laughing out loud when I reach for the door but grab the bottom chrome rung of a monster-truck ladder. Climb yourself on in up he-are, he drawls. I was so confused. We scamper up and ball into town in a monster truck, a little fuzzy teddy bear swinging from a ribbon clutched between rows of teeth below the driver's handlebar moustache. Now that I think of it, John Cusack did the same thing with a teddy bear in *Better off Dead.* She's out with this guy I know, I know it, he explains, shifting one gear too far for the speed limit. But she's gonna see how much I love her and she's gonna take me back when I find her. She'll see. I'll show her. He was pissed and shifting gears. It made me nervous as all get out. So that's just what we did, we got out, pronto. He'd been combing the streets of Penticton for hours hanging the teddy bear and wondering if he'd ever catch up with her. Me too. I sometimes wonder what happened to him. I sometimes wonder if anything happened to her. If I peer just over the edge of the last line of this story, all I see is a bit of grass where I slept beside my pile of tent poles that night.

*H*ere is what I liked to do with Brünhilde, my 1954 cream and red Austin. Waiting for the green light at Tenth and Alma, waiting to motor up the hill toward the UBC gates, I would see whether I was sitting beside a young driver guy in something other than an Austin. I would hold my left foot down on the clutch and gun the engine, or as we Austin drivers said, the motor, and look over at the guy and waggle my eyebrows. The verbal equivalent would have been: 'Wanna drag?' Then when the Alma light was yellow, I would hunch over the steering wheel and look straight ahead, intensely. When our light went green, the other guy would always zoom up the hill after a squeal of tires. Meanwhile, Brünhilde would be chugging across the intersection in low gear, which gear she would maintain most of the way up the hill. My passengers and I got a good laugh every time, and we didn't think the other guy ever felt all that foolish or angry. It was the kind of humour your mother ought to like – no cruelty, no violence. If I was alone, Brünhilde would make it up the hill in second gear, even with the weight in the back – a case of 40-weight motor oil. On the highway Brünhilde could do seventy miles on a quart of 40-weight motor oil.

I'll admit it here because nothing ever happened, but I drove for two jaw-clenching years tight-fisted and legally blind behind the wheel. Please feel free to take a moment for your uncomfortable pause. Yes, you should worry. At any given time there are Magoos out there who don't know they need to park it. If you go blind over a long period of time, and nobody has filled you in on this fact, then it doesn't seem like anything is out of the ordinary. The world still looks rosy by day, but maybe you begin to complain more often about ambient restaurant lighting and wonder what happened to the movie ushers with flashlights and pill-box hats. Or maybe you'd like to know why nobody else thinks the fog is really bad this fall. Looking back safe from the bus stop now, I can see how driving blind was more instructive than destructive for me. For example, I learned knowledge is not necessarily a matter of perception. I don't know about you, but I always feel safer when a driver pays attention to driving instead of, say, preening in the rear-view or toying with a couple of bozos revving Indy-happy at a red. Fiction is a marvellous prosthetic for perception. Because I couldn't see a thing at night, I learned quickly how to let my car tell me where I was and I learned not to give a damn about what I thought I knew was really going on out there. I was a clumsy waiter then, working nights in a dinky cafe in Langley. I'd drive home through the oily rain in my banged-up Acadian after a shift and swear every few blocks I was about to barrel into something. I couldn't see enough to say what that something was, but it persisted just ahead of my car, a blackness solid enough to do me in. Or maybe I thought I knew I was hogging the middle of the road or, worse, maybe I was about to digress down a sidewalk on some unsuspecting guy and his dog. But I couldn't tell, I didn't know, and at sixty kilometres an hour it was a bit uncomfortable not having any way of knowing where I was. That's why I listened to my car. I took my place as passenger on the roads with cat's eyes in the yellow line. I couldn't see them, of course (and didn't think anybody else could, for that matter) but they sure told me where I was when they went clunk clunk under the tires. 208th street in Langley is the first book I ever read in braille and the hero of that story got home safely every time I read it out loud.

*T*here was a time when I just naturally drove around the west. There were two times of day I liked best for driving the highway. At around five or five-thirty in the morning, when the sky was not really light yet and your headlights could still be seen a little on the pavement. There wasn't much traffic on the road, so the little there was, well, you all sort of acted as if you knew each other. The other time was in the evening when your radio picked up baseball games. You could drive for hours, getting concerned about the fate of the team you were now cheering for, or hoping, because there was no reason to shout, there in the car, especially if someone was asleep. This was so cozy. You might be hoping for Pocatello for the first time in your life, or it might be Medford. It didn't matter where you thought you were going – the real place was the gloaming on the well-broken-in road, and you felt as if you should always have known these American voices commenting on the nice night for baseball.

A—brief annotated list of made-for-TV cars:

1. *Dukes of Hazzard:* When I was ten we knew diddly-squat about General Lee or good old boys, what that Dixie flag meant or the numerous safety infractions our fathers faced if they welded shut the doors to the family station wagon.

2. *Wonderbug:* We always knew cars had faces.

3. *Starsky and Hutch:* When I played baseball in elementary school for the Simonds Stingers (the Simonds Stinkers), I sported a pair of knock-off Nikes. I took a lot of abuse over them, but I deftly argued that my sneakers were higher calibre footwear since, although the tip of the trademark swoosh was squished, the knock-off swoosh sufficiently resembled the white striping around the window and door of S&H's crime-fighting ride.

4. *Knight Rider:* The automated *Starsky and Hutch*, which happened to automate Hutch right out of the picture.

5. *Scooby-Doo:* A low-fi cabal for Generation X philosophers (see *Slacker* or *Jay and Silent Bob Strike Back*). But, who can resist? Why the hell didn't they have seats in the back of the Mystery Machine? It wasn't as if they were hauling around clunky carpet cleaning equipment from spooky abandoned house job to spooky abandoned house job.

6. *Speedbuggy:* We always knew cars had faces.

7. *The A-Team:* The eerie echo of Starsky and Hutch's famous stripe ran in red around Mr. T's Viet-vet van. Certainly better seating arrangements than the Mystery Machine, despite the heavy artillery lugged from spooky abandoned town job to spooky abandoned town job.

8. *Herbie, the Love Bug: Wonderbug* for squares, man.

9. *Smokey and the Bandit* (Parts 1–48): The Bandit must have been some inbred relative of the Duke family with that similar genetic perfection for finding bridges under construction.

10. *Batman:* A practical metropolitan crime-fighting car. Sure you want a convertible to show off your superhero images while zooming about Gotham in a hurry, but that red emergency light mounted between the dynamic duo must've been essential for shoving rushhour traffic aside or KAPLOWY!

*B*y now it is just about universally agreed that 1948 was the greatest year in the history of civilization. Partly this has to do with Dior, partly with the Cleveland Indians' pitching rotation, partly even with *The Treasure of the Sierra Madre*. Plus this: have you had a relaxed look at a 1948 Mercury coupé? They can try all they want to but they will never make an automobile that looks as good as that. Especially if it is that dark blue that looks a little purple in the dry Okanagan sunlight. Were they ever any other colour? Anyway – in the summer of 1949 I loaded up my Baby Brownie and went all around Oliver and environs taking pictures of every kind of 1948 car I could find. Sometimes I had to wait for tourists or visiting baseball players to stop in town. I had to wait till 1949 because hardly anyone in Oliver ever had a brand new car. My father had quite a few cars, one after the other, but he never in his life had a brand new car. I still have those square black and white snapshots, a couple dozen of them. I'll bet that half of those car names don't exist any more. I was a camera boy when I was twelve. A lot of the less intelligent boys in Oliver were nuts about cars. I wasn't interested in the cars – just the pictures of the cars.

August 22, 1988

To: WAREHOUSE SHIPPING/RECEIVING DEPARTMENT
Re: FORKLIFT ABUSE

Please post these rules on the forklift steering consoles and in your lunchroom.

Thank you,
Moe Jarvis
Production Supervisor
Pacific West Pools and Spas

ALL EMPLOYEES ARE REQUESTED TO COMPLY WITH THE FOLLOWING:

1. Please do not play 'joust' with the forklifts. Ryan fell off No. 2 last week, as some of you know.
2. Please do not ask Ryan to stand on the forks and pull heavy objects from the warehouse racking. He has not fallen yet but other heavy objects have. This is dangerous for employees working on the warehouse floor.
3. Please check that the propane tank is turned on before telling staff the forklift is broken. If help is required, contact Dave in the machine shop before phoning outside the company for assistance. This includes your father, Ryan.
4. Please do not snip the ignition wire and poke the two live ends out from under the driver's seat. Ryan was very close to quitting after he turned the key. A plastic roof has been taped to the frame to keep as much water as possible from pooling on the seat.
5. Please do not hide the forklift keys from Ryan.
6. Please do not leave the forks raised when the forklift is not in use, especially at the end of a shift. This includes leaving the forks raised under Ryan's car. Again, please do not hide the keys.

The second car I ever owned cost one and a half times what my first car cost; i.e., it set me back $150. It was a 1947 Pontiac[1] with white-wall tires, so it was only fifteen years old. I can imagine who had it before me. It was, I guess, chopped and channelled. The rear window was only inches high. The car lay close to the pavement, and it was a kind of rust-red primer-paint colour.[2] The guy had moved the gearshift around to the left side of the steering column, so you had to learn the gears upside down. I suppose this freed your right arm and hand for attention to your date. Very cool, I guess. He had also affixed a knuckle-duster to the big steering wheel. This device was illegal, I'd always heard, but after you got used to grabbing it and making big circles with it, it seemed to make steering easier. Once, two blocks east of where I live now, a guy came speeding over a rise to my right and pranged[3] into my right front fender, next to where my date Angela was sitting. During the subsequent proceedings some cop or some lawyer made a remark about how the asshole[4] was always driving like that. When spring was coming to an end, my second gear quit working and so did the front brakes. Nevertheless, I put all my worldly possessions inside this dented Pontiac and drove it over the Hope-Princeton mountain pass to Oliver. The highway reaches heights above 1200 metres[5] three times at least, and my radiator was no great shakes, either. When I got to Oliver I had a photograph taken that seems to show me making the big dent in the fender with my kid brother's head. This kind of car didn't seem to attract much attention in the Interior, but back in Vancouver I would get pulled over by the cops every Saturday night because this was such a suspicious-looking vehicle. And me just a literature boy in horn-rimmed glasses.

---

1 Chief of the Ottawa people, he was the Native commander during the Pontiac War, 1763–4.
2 Base, sealer, or the like.
3 In the RCAF in the Fifties, airplane crashes were called 'prangs.'
4 Term generally applied to another driver, even in normal traffic.
5 We used feet in those days. Say a little over 4000 feet.

I think it's important to pause for a moment and explain to the patient reader why this book may feel lopsided. Actually, it's only lopsided in being written, not in the writing. In March of 2001 George wouldn't dare to eat the terrific sushi at Koko's the night we cooked up this book, but he agreed heartily that he would dare to write fifty single-page car stories – what we affectionately refer to as our car panels. How's your car, GB? Chugging along. How's yours, Blind Ryan? Racing past. It is now October 9th and I'm stalled in the middle of classes at the college about comma or coma splices. Yet, despite the constraint, I am still managing to bang out a car panel here and there. You probably can't tell from the book, but I've finished thirty-eight of my fifty. You might think the ever-compulsive and sporty George is gunning ahead or pulling up the rear, but I think it's important to pause and note that at this stage of the writing he has only fifteen panels to his name. I'm sure we could blame retirement for that, or maybe it's Canadian History weighing down the keyboard. What I do know is that George tells a good story about the time many years ago when he was driving late at night in the hot Okanagan summer. GB was doing his usual best to get there on time, being a man who believes in punctuality and punctuation. But the late hour and warm Okanagan was heavy on his noggin. So sleepy GB did what is natural to poets and fell asleep at the wheel. What saved our author from off-roading through a nearby peach orchard was the radio. Radios are often in his poetry and often in his sleep. The opening scat from Little Richard's 'Tutti Frutti' belted from GB's tuner and snapped him back into consciousness. Little Richard, as he will tell you, saved his life, but not in the late Little Salvation Richard way. This all still sounds a bit fishy to me. I'm also well aware that Cocteau's radio continues to insist poets are liars. That's the program we're listening to. But let's pause for a commercial break to announce it is now thirty-nine to fifteen in the panel count. Better catch up, George – I'm one more ahead and it was YOURS! In other words, A-WOP-BA-BALLOO-BOP BA-LOP-BAM-BOOM!

In later years Frank Davey was always going with my wife Angela to help her buy antique furniture because he was good at that. But – well, not but, I guess, but well – several decades ago he went with me to help me buy my first car, because I had no idea how to do such a thing. I knew how to publish or rather type a poetry magazine, but I had no idea how you purchased an automobile. Out we went in his car – I am always forgetting what it was, even though I was in it when it turned over in a snow-storm in the State of Washington – to Kingsway. We went look-ing at one of the used car lots with no building but maybe a little portable shack and a lot of plastic pennants, really awful colours, on diagonal strings overhead. I looked at this and I looked at that, and for the first time in my life I experienced that itchy thrill of almost having a car of your own. And when I gave them a hundred dollars and did some minimal paperwork I don't remember, I had my first car. It was a black 1941 Chevrolet with a little old clock on the high dashboard and chrome along the outside. The headlights both came on when you used the switch. It also had a spotlight, which was illegal if you weren't a cop with a cop car. The spotlight was big and powerful and sent a beam of light deep into anyone's back yard. It was right outside the driver's window and I was the driver for a change. In Vancouver every Friday or Saturday night the cops would pull me over to see what kind of guy was driving this black car with a spotlight. But my favourite memory of that car was driving up Dunbar Street with my white silk scarf on and Angela Luoma by my side. When it was time to dispense with this shiny black car I left it in front of the Salvation Army store off Twelfth and Kingsway, I think it was.

$\mathcal{S}$omeone who has never stepped a well-shod foot beyond Vancouver's Robson Street will be less familiar with a curious tradition of car museums along the sides of many roads commonly known in the vernacular as 'ditches.' Ditches are where you find surprised drivers and their cars propped by this earthy plinth at odd angles for the amusement or shock of passing traffic. One of my earliest memories is from the perspective of my mother's ditched Toyota, the headlights aimed up at the sharp winter sun like a would-be space shuttle. Even if you proceed with caution on an old South Langley road, black ice will at any moment reach out with its key and quietly shut off your tires. Before you spin off into Oz, before you are sent into orbit like one of the many moons tumbling about Uranus, there's a moment of eerie silence underneath the all-seasons, just enough for your mother to lever an uh oh and lower her train-crossing arm in front of little you in your passenger's seat. Then there's the whirl, then the confusion, then the abrupt landing, then the winter sky. Then I think my father pulled us out of the ditch, or helped us out of the car. A man was there, in any case, and my own curating of historical order suggests it was my father just before he was my father. At that time in the seventies Ma and I lived in a basement suite in South Langley and somewhere along the way she stopped and married my father. Then he was called Miles. So far he hadn't been around that long, but Miles married my Ma in the not-too-distant future from that point in the ditch. I was too young to know, so it was flat-out disorienting the next summer at Pender Harbour when, while fishing off the docks for bottom feeders, Miles said I could call him Dad now if I wanted to. I didn't have anything to say, though, so we stood listening to that eerie silence, the kind you hear when the tires lose their grip. The way you rescue yourself, I learned, is you make something up. Uh, Dad? I asked. Yeah, as he dropped his hook in the water. Uh, um, what time is it ... Dad? He looked at his watch. About two o'clock. That was it. With that came a permanent change in perspective. I think that's the first time I felt language actually work. I felt a new word take to the world and it actually had some grip. At the age of four I really couldn't have cared less what time it was, but I sure knew where we were when we spent that afternoon sun on the dock's edge spinning our reels.

In the late summer of 1963, we moved to Calgary for my first full-time teaching job, at the University of Alberta at Calgary. I was also super of the apartment building we lived in so we could afford our semi-basement suite. At the university I was responsible to Earl Guy, our department chairman. At the apartment I was responsible to Arnie Dworkin. His family owned apartment buildings in Calgary, and the rumour was that he took his German shepherd with him when he went around to collect rents. I had a block heater put into my 1954 Chevrolet Bel Air. In October I went to Tucson to be the poet at University of Arizona for a week. Down there I told them that up in Alberta we plug in our cars overnight and whenever we are not using them. Ha ha ha ha, they replied. When I got onto the plane in Tucson it was ninety degrees. When I got off the plane in Calgary it was below freezing.

Summer holidays were always high-maintenance for my parents. Having four kids and three jobs to manage between them, there wasn't much time or energy unaccounted for. I seem to recall my strategy was to hang around the kitchen and complain of Absolutely Nothing To Do in order to get an inroad with my father. If it worked, poor Ma would finally give. Why don't you go outside and help Dad work on the car? Yes. Now I couldn't be sent back. In our driveway at that time was a lime green Maverick. I didn't know the first thing about engines and it remains that way. This isn't something I'm proud of, like some eggheads are, but I've never been able to move beyond my hazy sense of the theory behind an engine to its manipulation and repair. But I was a curious kid, so I went outside happily on several summer afternoons to work on the car, or at least to find out what that meant. Although I was curious, I still suffered the distractions of early-teen image-consciousness, which required I first go downstairs and unhook my Realistic-brand ghetto blaster, choose a handful of decent male-bonding tapes and take the lot outside for reassembly. I suppose in my imagination I saw my father and I with our grease-smeared faces under the Maverick's rusting hood, tapping screwdrivers in time to 'Rebel Yell' as we discussed the possible origins of a phantom noise. In my imagination, the music and curious pose over the engine would inevitably lead to the kind of secret knowledge and horsing around I'd seen between my dad and the other men he worked with in the machine shop. But leaning against the car in the hot sun, I'd watch my dad for a good hour feigning comprehension. Later, or, rather, recently, my parents attended a handful of my poetry readings. I suspect they didn't want to go all that much (and I can't say as I blame them). I'm sure I caught my dad kind of into it at times, drinking beer with him in the back alley and smoking cigarettes, talking art, kind of. There he told me how he gave my first book to his boss and his boss said, I don't get it, but I'm impressed. I like to imagine them looking at it in the shop, trying to figure out what the big fuss is. I always was impressed, too. The engine always turned over. Always to school on time. To work. Cars and poetry and their phantom noises. That's the difference, the question of family.

*W*ell, Willy and I were in the back of the car, my father driving and my mother also up front. Now, Willy and I had been trying to figure out how the sunset works on a moon of Uranus, and where west is. Because Uranus tumbles along its trip around the sun – i.e., its orbit is on the same plane as its rotation, and then it has a number of moons, all of them but one going around in the same direction as it tumbles. We were wondering about that moon that goes the other way. Well, you can imagine how hard this was to get a hold of while in a car on the way to Penticton. A little later my mother said, 'It's not the going there that I mind; it's the getting there.' Willy and I started a conversation about that. Should it be 'It's not the getting there I mind; it's the going there,' or the way my mother had it. We went on and on, arguing in great deal. Then my mother said, 'Let's talk about the hemisphere,' meaning the stuff we were onto earlier.

*W*hen my dad sold my first car for $300, he dumped it on an unsuspecting kid who thought it was a steal. My little brother, Rory, never looked at my dad the same, I suspect. Rory saw him at that moment as two-faced. He couldn't understand how Dad could sell a car to someone without telling that person the truth: it was a piece of shit. The car dropped oil like bread crumbs and there was a hole – well, a trap door – rusting away right under the driver's seat. To sell it, we parked my little blue Valdez in a fresh spot every time. No evidence of oil there, at least not like the tar sands deepening across the street where I usually parked. And who looks under the driver's seat unless you drop a significant amount of money, a burning cigarette, or something else you might be smoking in a City Park shady spot? Rory thought, for a short time, that my dad had done something horribly immoral. But it couldn't last. Dad was Rory's hero, and sacrificing a part of one's purity to the system seemed to Rory to be part of what makes a hero. It gives the hero a bit of sadness and humility, enough for us to admire and justify our hopes we will grow up to be just like our heroes. Take a look at car ads for proof. It should be no surprise that Lindsay Wagner sells cars. When I think about the Bionic Woman, I have to wonder which half of her human-and-artificial system interface made for heroism. If Rory asked me a weird question like that, I couldn't rightly answer, but I'd wish I could answer him.

I can never remember whether Waterman's Hill is the road going up out of OK Falls or the road coming down into Penticton. We were going up the curvy hill out of OK Falls, my dad driving, my mother in the front seat beside him. I don't know where the rest of us were exactly, except my baby brother Jimmy. I can remember him because he opened the left rear door and there was the surface of the road going by and it looked as if he were going to step right out, probably didn't even understand that we were moving. I don't know what we were doing, probably about 40 mph, and turning a little to the right and still climbing. My dad kept on driving, but as he did so he reached behind him over the seat with his left arm and grabbed little Jimmy by the arm and yanked him back into the car and closed the door and kept the car on the right side of the road, and we drove on to Penticton or Naramata. I was in the back of the car, and while all this stuff was happening so fast I hadn't had time to do anything but see what was happening. It was just like the time my other little brother fell head first into the excavation, or the time the kitchen door closed on the kitten's neck and my dad had to take it out of my sight to the garage. I just saw these things happening. This was just another way in which my dad was clearly better than me.

I remember David Hasselhoff in *Knight Rider*. He played mysterious crime fighter Michael Knight, and his faithful sidekick, a friendly black Pontiac Trans Am, was played by – er – a friendly black Pontiac Trans Am. KITT was the car's name, which stood for the Knight Industries Two Thousand. What a brand that was. Sadly, it's 2002 and I'm still looking for KITT. The most astonishing thing about this car was how it talked to Michael Knight and was, like most memorable chums, a pretty good listener to boot. I don't mean in a water-cooler-casual sort of way. Sure, their conversations kept Michael's jaw-jutting machismo company on their various car-oriented misadventures, but if Michael Knight got in hot water over his mullet, he just had to call for help and KITT would drive real fast to rescue our hero in a car-oriented way. Then a woe-begotten Michael Knight would get inside his warm sidekick and KITT would promptly say something comforting and witty in his fatherly British way, something like 'Michael! I couldn't find you anywhere and, indeed, my bio-radar sensory systems were overloading with worry.' Now, I never did get a Pontiac Trans Am, but I got the next best thing in going blind. Instead of KITT, I have a computer who talks to me. I can make him say witty and comforting things, too. Listen: 'My bio-radar sensory systems were overloading with worry.' The similarities are uncanny, eh? What's different, though, is KITT was terrific at mapping things out. KITT could spot a menacing gang of vaguely Eastern-European commie conspirators way down the road, judge the situation, then drive over them all with four-wheeled justice. It's because the car had this red Cyclops eye on the grill which looked back and forth just like a Cylon in *Battlestar Galactica*. My computer and I aren't quite there yet. He's inept at telling me where I'm going. In fact, he only reads what's already been typed. There's KITT, out in the world, driving ahead, and my computer's stuck reading the script back to me. So you'd think if they can design a car like KITT, or make a computerized voice for the blind, then it shouldn't be all that fictional to imagine some corporation by now would have cooked up a better solution for getting blind folks around this ouch ouch rigid world. I mean, nobody has improved on swinging a very un-sexy white stick with some red tape from side to side. Amazing to think that's as far down the road as that technology's gone.

*B*ehold the chariot of the Fairy Queen! Celestial coursers paw the unyielding air. Their filmy pennons at her word they furl, and stop obedient to the reins of light. These the Queen of Spells drew in. She spread a charm around the spot, and, leaning graceful from the ethereal car, long did she gaze, and silently, upon the slumbering maid.

I used to work at the pool factory with an old man named … what was his name? He spoke English with a Polish accent so heavy it crushed his English into little bits and pieces. One of the only words we could usually grab out of the rubble was 'fackin,' and boy he said fackin a lot. Fackin this and fackin that. Oh, and 'vee hell,' which tended to follow fackin. Together these made his favourite expletive. I might say to him one day, 'Hey, I can't find the forklift keys anywhere,' and then he might throw up his arms and exclaim, 'Oh, fackin vee hell.' I still can't remember his name, so let's call him Marshall McLuhan, or Fackin Marshall for short. Old Fackin Marshall knew how to bend language in more bizarre and effective ways than I could ever hope. For example, often machinery would quit working on him and Fackin Marshall would say something like, 'Fackin vee hella, this vee crappered shit.' He was a real neat guy to talk to. One day my boss asked me to help Fackin Marshall deliver a dozen aluminum sides for a pool we were building in Mission. I liked driving with him. Fackin Marshall told me how fackin fast this fackin job would be. Well, I think that's what he said. This job site was a pool-shaped mud puddle dug twelve feet deep at the bottom of a lengthy and steep z-shaped driveway. Now, here's the approach. Fackin Marshall understood his job not as a delivery driver required to unbind and unload the van's contents, but as an on-site time/space engineer. A dozen aluminum panels, each about ten feet long, required we clip the banding and unload one at a time, one man on each end. It looked like a good fifteen minutes to carry each between the van and the pool floor. This was too much time and space for old Fackin Marshall so, instead, the fackin guy clipped the banding wire, slid open the van's back door and drove back up the driveway mumbling in an annoyed way. Two minutes later the van roared in reverse back down the driveway, zigged and zagged crinkum-crankum with the road, locked its brakes and skidded to a halt just a few feet shy of the would-be pool's edge. Nine or ten of the aluminum sides shot from the back of the van and landed in various shapes of crumpled at the bottom of the hole. This was an important cautionary tale for me. Fackin Marshall thought he could collapse some time but hadn't stop to notice aluminum isn't quite as strong in vee hell.

*I*t was those two damned women novelists from eastern Australia, trying to get me into trouble. Hell with it, I'm going to mention their names: Jean Bedford and Georgia Savage. I should have known what kind of girls they were when I heard them badmouthing each other to the handsome African poet. They just wanted to have fun, those two. So in the bar in Perth, where I saved the life of another Australian fiction writer the night before, they told me that when an Aussie is having a drink he lifts his glass and says 'Up your leg' to his drinking buddies. It was just my luck that a little later Doris Lessing came into the bar and sat straight in a chair against the wall and held a glass of water. She has braids on her head in real life, too. Naturally, I raised my glass and said 'Up your leg' to Doris Lessing. Oh boy. Just about that time it dawned on me that those horrible women had set me up so they could raise their glasses and say 'Up yours, too!' Now here is how this becomes a car panel or whatever we end up calling these things. The next day Doris Lessing and I shared a taxi cab to the airport. She was going down to the bottom left corner of Australia to see the varieties of gum trees down there, she said. I was going to Sydney to catch a plane to Wellington. It is a long drive to the airport from Perth, and I had been there once before. So on the way I pointed toward a road that marched off to our left. 'That,' I announced, 'is the road to the Western Australia baseball stadium.' 'Oh, really?' inquired Ms Lessing.

It's been observed that a Harley Davidson ceases to be a means of transportation when it hangs from a theme-restaurant ceiling. Hanging there, it announces its true character in the theatre of a culture's mythology. That Hog is more than its tenacious ability to move a bearded passenger from macho point A to macho point B. *Moby Dick*, I suspect, makes a similar case for a whale. I've never read the novel and, frankly, remain embarrassed to admit it, but I did sit through *Corvette Summer* at least half a dozen times. If you don't remember this ungodly odyssey, it starred Mark Hamill of Luke Skywalker fame just shortly after his X-Wing fighter celebrity sputtered and crashed somewhere just shy of the Universal Studio gates. Hamill played an aspiring and gifted teenage grease monkey. An Einstein of shop class, Hamill and some buddies built a super Corvette of indescribable aesthetic failure. This thing had pipes and intakes and chrome and all sorts of shit popping in and out of the body. This was the Platonic Corvette – the Corvette from which all other permutations could be derived. Now, the dramatic arc of this story begins when the car – let's call it Moby Dick – is stolen from Hamill the first night he takes it out on the road. The journey to find this stolen beast then takes Hamill across the country to Las Vegas where, after a series of rumoured sightings and phantom glimpses, he finally tracks Moby Dick down in a Vegas showroom, slightly altered and painted a clean, shining white, but unmistakably the overdone labour of an aspiring and gifted teenage grease monkey. I can't quite remember now, but I'd bet my last Vegas dollar the car is destroyed in the fight for ownership. We've seen this story before and we know nobody's gonna get the girl in the end. I mean the car. I'm only so sure about this because a car ceases to be a car when it runs around inside a familiar narrative like this one, and the point was to make this car beyond car-ness for Hamill, just like that Harley. The mythic nature of Hamill's Moby Dick precipitates a low-fi lighting-out to see the country, to go west, young man. So it makes sense our grease monkey can't find the car in the end. I've summarized this movie to a number of my bookwormy friends, some of whom have read *Moby Dick*, but not one of them will fess up to having seen this flick and its tale.

*L*ast night my daughter and I watched *The Blue Dahlia,* and though it was written by Raymond Chandler, the studio must have told him to dumb it down, because it just wasn't as good as it used to be. When I was a kid my favourite male movie star was Alan Ladd. But boy, he was a lousy actor. He wasn't even any good in all those fist fights. But *The Blue Dahlia,* which for a while I got mixed up with *The Glass Key.* The film was released in 1946, and it seems to take place late in World War II, even late for the US version of World War II. Yet all the cars are brand new and very clean, and nifty. For example, Veronica Lake's car is a two-tone convertible with leather seats. I think that 1941 was the last year for new cars. When I was a kid in Lawrence, BC, a brand-new car was something that would bring boys and some dads running from all directions. Maybe everyone in California had nifty new cars. All these movies took place in California, and cars and telephones and hats were very important. If you looked at the cars parked on the streets in these movies, they were all brand new, even in 1945. I can't imagine my dad or Gordon Bauer's dad driving a brand-new car, and I can't imagine Brian Donlevy driving anything else. The only person driving a jalopy would be a skinny old farmer guy who gets in the way.

*A*t seventeen I had a good tan from working all summer in the shipping department of a Langley warehouse. The company manufactured swimming pools and hot tubs. They sold everything from the water-softening chemical dust that burned my eyes once to the 300 pounds of blue vinyl pool lining a novice forklift jockey dropped on my foot. All this encouraged my boss to think I was accident prone. A mustachioed born-again, my boss's upper lip twitched with hairy meditation. His minivan sported a personalized SRVIVR license plate, after all, so he was both wary and understanding of my desire to drive deliveries the day I passed my driver's test. I just thought driving deliveries a cherry job. It meant smoking in the cab, being on the road with the radio on, windows down, drive-thru food at your side, that sort of stuff. Beat the hell out of wrapping aluminum liner edges in plastic all afternoon. That stuff was actually called 'coping.' Knighton! Your turn to do the coping! SRVIVR bossman gave me a reluctant go-ahead, and within four hours of his consent I did an efficient $8000 in damage. Here's the breakdown, as it were. First, I drove to Whiterock with about a dozen lengths of PVC pipe bundled to my roof. I didn't notice the guy in front of me brake for a four-way stop and had to lock up my wheels, launching a dozen pipes over his car into the intersection where they piled up like the super-size fries around my feet. Pick 'em up fast. Honks. Fuck yous. Now I'm late. I made for stop number two, the engine screaming with SRVIVR pride. After two blocks of pride I took off the passenger-side mirror on a mailbox. The mailbox went, too, but I didn't stop, I was late to pick up four hot tub shells in Surrey. There the guys stacked them upside down on top of each other on my flatbed with a Cat in the Hat lean. Then about a mile down the road I noticed the straps dangling festively from the sides of the truck. All four hot tubs bounced on deck just a couple of feet from bouncing off. Pull over. Emergency lights. Shove and strap 'em. Honks. Fuck yous. I'm just taking my knocks, I thought. Pull away, lots of pride. Zipped back to the warehouse and dumped my leaning tower of tubs in the parking lot. I wasn't allowed to drive deliveries any more. I pleaded my case, though, always the SRVIVR. Although it costs, I think it's upon us SRVIVRs to forgive with charity our transgressions, don't you think? Pink slip. Coping. Next summer we were dancing in night clubs to 'Jesus Built my Hotrod' and I was a nervous waiter.

I used to do that all the time. I would be stopped at a red light, and there you would be, you could use both hands, I would take out a cigarette and push in the lighter. Now this usually happened at Cambie Street. The lights at Cambie take forever, especially 41st at Cambie and 33rd at Cambie, so the lighter has time to get red hot and pop out, I always thought it looked like a little toaster or the element on a stove. The lighter pops out and you step on the gas. This is really hard for a layman to understand. You hear a sound inside the car and assume that the colour of the light up there has changed. But it was one of the recurring reasons to quit smoking. If the traffic is heavy, smoking can kill you.

I shared a cab once with Jean-Paul Sartre in Pusan, South Korea, to help him look for Christmas trees. Professor Kim from the city university sat low in the back seat with Jean-Paul, the Korean professor's Superman baseball cap pulled down low on his brow. The three of us had just visited a small Buddhist shrine maintained by Professor Kim's lovely niece. She read Jean-Paul's numbers, declared we would all be surprised by our quest, and returned to the adjacent room. How pleased we were. We followed and watched her resume poking a young student. Acupuncture, she explained, is an excellent way to prepare for university exams. Professor Kim nodded with approval. Stretched on his belly, the student rested his chin on a pillow. Long needles stood at attention on his back while he watched a *M*A*S*H* rerun. When he giggled, the pins quivered like a grove of gumtrees in a heavy wind. Soon the three of us left Professor Kim's niece to her work, flagging down the only taxi we saw. In fact, it was the only car on the winding mountain road we'd ever seen. 'Kom-up sam ni da,' offered Jean-Paul gratefully as he settled into the back seat and dusted the skiff of snow from his chapeau. As we drove, Jean-Paul told the story of his day in the Nampo-dong market. Professor Kim had introduced Jean-Paul to a young student of letters and the young poet's father. The father and son stood next to a brand new car, a Hyundai, of course, a graduation present. The son beamed with pride. In the driver's seat a freshly severed pig's head grinned. You could feel evil spirits flee the scene with bloody-head dispatch, grinned Jean Paul. When we arrived at his preferred forest, he flipped the cabbie a 10,000-won tip and hoisted our equipment from the trunk. Outside in the mountain air, strolling through the trees in search of just the right Christmas arbre, Jean-Paul stepped carefully ahead, sweeping the ground for old landmines. Then, as they say, all of a sudden … Alright, alright, I'm just kidding. I was never in Pusan looking for Christmas cheer with Jean-Paul Sartre. Just joshing. But, seriously, did I ever tell you about the time, under the gumtrees and moonlight, I cuddled up next to Doris Lessing in a backseat way?

I've always been a snob about car songs. Could never sing them or listen to them. I mean, come on – singing about your car? How is this any better than the TV commercials for cars? How is this any better than that annoying US song about 'they ran through the bushes'? Little Deuce Coupe. I never even knew what that meant – maybe a two-seater? I don't know. Oh, Maybelline, why can't you be true – that song made me think quite a bit less of Chuck Berry. I didn't mind hey little schoolgirl or whatever, but a car with a girlfriend's funny name? A lot of those car songs were about racing with some rival's car or some outlaw car. I thought that was pretty crude. I mean what sort of mind do you have if you sing a love song to your transportation? Ode to Freedom, says Percy Shelley. Cadillac doin' 'bout hundred and five, sings a loutish voice from our near past. That heavy-drinking young woman from the sixties blew it for me for good when she squealed for a Mercedes-Benz. I mean, those old country and western freight trains and their whistles are just tolerable. Those trucker CB radio songs from the seventies were juked by guys with huge belt buckles and ugly sideburns. There's the odd Greyhound bus song, not so bad because they just disappear. Hardly anyone bothers to sing about Boeing jets because you don't have an interesting tale to tell if you can afford airfare. But what about all those forgotten singing groups that named themselves after cars – the Cadillacs or the Mustangs or the Bel Airs, maybe? Remember those homemade-looking album covers in bad colours? Then remember those album covers with easy-looking women draped over the hood of some muscle car? Makes you want to puke. Worse than being carsick. See the world today, in your Chevrolet, asshole.

When George turned the ignition we were surprised

Not Amiri Baraka, but Public Enemy because

This makes George public enemy #2 behind the wheel, for example,

It's sad but politics are cheaper than cars, particularly good ones. Then

nervous guys threaten to meet by the bike racks after school.

Necropolis behind the wheel.

for the road. Just slow down or

Steer your partner round and round, fight the power till

to feel a growl of power rise and encircle us.

I got the tape for $3.50 and I like their politics.

I listen with a racing heart when George Stanley says, 'Ram him!'

cars are cheaper than death, and because they go together often enough

I really wish George Stanley drove like the wind.

Metropolis cops a feel

go down, motor over to the hoedown, listen, Bro:

that sound is found, I mean REV that hour, driver.

*M*y top ten favourite car songs today:

'Cars,' Gary Numan
'Small Car,' Marvin Pontiac
'(Oh Lord, won't you buy me a) Mercedes-Benz,' Janis Joplin
'Brand New Cadillac,' the Clash version
'Jaguar and Thunderbird,' The Troggs
'The Passenger,' Iggy Pop
'Little Red Corvette,' Prince
'Jesus Built My Hotrod,' Ministry
'Car Wash,' Rose Royce
'One Piece at a Time,' Johnny Cash

There were two things that were naturally frightening about my father's grey four-door 1936 Ford. Well, it was either a Ford or a Chev. I was always carsick when we went to Summerland or Penticton, so my mother put the slick cold brown paper next to my chest skin. This is not repetition, this is continuity. Big inside of the dark winter car, and you like to remember it as warm, but really it was cold, and if you were lucky you got a robe or a blanket or an overcoat to curl up under, but then the colder you were the less carsick, so your mother thought it was worth it to let you roll your window down, though you recognized your father's stoicism and the back of his head. How come your sister never got carsick, never had to puke out the window and along the side of the car (as I did years later in the taxi in downtown Auckland). That, and she got naturally curly hair. And she won a prize for her costume in the parade, a bride, for heaven's sake. The first frightening thing. It was still wartime and we lived in a soldier's house in an orchard, with a long gravel driveway to Route 97. One time my dad had to drive somewhere, into Oliver, probably. I stood on the back bumper and held onto the trunk door, I guess. I thought to steal a ride to the end of the driveway, but now he was going faster and faster and crunching over the gravel. I didn't know that he was going for sure to stop before turning onto the highway. Had to make this choice, let go and not get foot tangled and roll hard in the gravel. Then not go for pity to my mum, because I'd be in trouble, you see? The second. My dad came home, and it was my sister's turn or job to bring his briefcase from the car. So I pretended to go for it, and she scrambled as fast as she could, this girl, and managed to slam her little finger in the car door. It cut the end of her finger right off, except a hanging bit of skin. So we drove in this car three miles into town to Dr Cope, and yes, he did sew it back on. I felt terrible, but it was worse than that – they thought I'd slammed the car door on her finger. I don't remember how long it was that they thought I'd done it. And anyway, it was in a way as bad as if I had. But really, I was innocent, really.

*L*ike a handful of gumbooted kids in Langley, I learned to drive when I was ten. We'd drive about ten minutes from my family's cul-de-sac to my grandparents' farm every Sunday for dinner. On a summer day that year my father taught me to drive on my grandfather's 1952 Ford 9N tractor. At ten there is no distinction between a tractor and a car. This wasn't *Knight Rider* by a long shot, but it had an engine, a gearshift (two gears and reverse) and I got to steer the works. What's this for? I asked, pointing to a red ball on the steering wheel. That's the suicide grip, my father prophesied. We drove slowly in low gear toward the wooded back acreage with me behind the wheel and my father standing behind me on the tractor's hitch. Comforted I could steer a straight line, he allowed me to depress the clutch and shift into high gear. The clutch went down down down under my short suburban leg. Feeling for the clutch bottom, I must have looked like I was pedalling this four-wheeled antique, leaning precariously to one side of the seat. In high gear on a raised dirt trail we approached the bridge across my grandparents' pond. The bridge wasn't there and now the pond was fenced off. Brake and we'll turn around, my father said. I leaned and pressed again, looking for the bottom of the clutch. Brake! he ordered but I couldn't reach the bottom of the clutch on one side and the bottom of the brake on the other. Well, some poets claim the shift into modernity happened when art ceased to attempt copies of nature, instead imitating nature in the act of composition itself. But in 1982 I didn't know much about nature. I knew *Knight Rider*, though, and the impression I got from that show was you stopped a speeding car by veering hard on the wheel, which apparently causes a car to skid to a very cool halt. So I did just that. I veered hard to the left, spinning the suicide grip with veteran ease, and consequently sped Grandpa's 1952 9N directly into a sturdy tree. My driving impressed the tractor's grill into the tree's trunk. I looked back at the image with secret pride while dad drove us home to Sunday dinner. Eventually that tree grew over my first contact with modernity and something like art, if not Impressionism.

𝓘 guess that a lot of boys in the Okanagan Valley learned to drive on tractors. You've been working in the orchard for a few years, and eventually some adult gets really busy doing something else and asks you to bring or take the tractor, maybe with a half a trailer load, somewhere. I learned on a little Ford tractor in an orchard up past the airstrip. Was it red or green or grey? But it would be on Aikens's big orchard above Naramata that I really got going. Uncle Gerry and my father went on a hunting trip, and I was left in charge of the big grey Oliver tractor. It had only one wheel in front and huge back tires filled with water. My Uncle Gerry was the ramrod of Aikens's orchard, and he could have left the Irish guy with the upside-down pipe, Paddy, or someone else to run the tractor. But I got the job. I think they were making me grow up. Forty-five years later I would buy a first-edition Gertrude Stein book in a store in Penticton, and it would have John Aikens's signature in it. Well, it was probably the second day when I backed over something sharp and one of the big tires sprang a leak. Now this was the kind of thing that was always happening to me. In the air force I accidentally dyed my gym t-shirt pink and I didn't know it, for example, until the corporal started yelling at me. I was always catching trouble when it wasn't really my fault. But this turned out pretty neat, because what Paddy did was to show me how to operate the old yellow tractor with lugs instead of tires and levers instead of a steering wheel. To turn hard left between trees, you'd brake the left track and turn on a dime. It was like driving a little tank, and I just now remember the satisfactory clanking and grinding noises and the loud exhaust that pointed straight up. It was so complicated and so enjoyable to back up with a trailer piled high with props on tilted ground around some trees on the edge of a clay cliff with Lake Okanagan below. Who would have thought that work could be so enjoyable? But a week later Uncle Gerry and my dad came back and I had to pick pears.

*O*kay, I'll do it. She thought her car would be big enough for the both of us and I agreed because I couldn't say I didn't know yet. What I learned, I think, is how the material world in all its superficially pleasing forms sometimes constrains the nature of human contact in unnatural ways. I was nervous as we trawled Langley for a quiet, dark and secluded place to park. Suburbs don't make many of these. There we light all the corners so nothing can be discovered or concealed. She was tiny and brown-haired in a big boat of a car, eyes dashing about just above the dash. That's my high school there, next to the Christian Life Assembly. We parked and rearranged space for ourselves, two tiny figures in a big Ford in the eye of a bigger empty parking lot. If you can't hide, we reasoned, overexpose yourself. Borges once peered through his dead eyes and saw that a wide open desert is the worst labyrinth. That's swell, but I couldn't even figure us out in a car. In the front seat, bums hung awkwardly up in the air with nowhere to land, feet fought with the radio knobs, the gearshift repeatedly poked and tapped us like a needy brat. Into the back we climbed, trying with seats tipped forward and tipped back, heads down for modesty, then doors open for that extra inch. Sit up, she said, and maybe turn around. Okay, and put your legs thataway, I suggested. And what about this, she engineered, does that work? We worked together on the problem of sex and our material reality but wanted too much from her car. It was too much with us. Maybe even as much with us as the police cruiser that pulled up next to our first time. The constable got out of his car as we got into our Levis. A knowing moon face leaned in the car window. Evening, it said, and shined a light around the car's busy interior. What you kids up to? he asked. Not too much, I said, not too much at all. Karen and I broke up not long after that. Then about a year later we bumped into each other at a Vancouver night spot called Luv-A-Fair. It was eighties retro night, of course. I'd just moved into my first apartment and didn't have much money or stuff. Less stuff the better, I thought. I'll give you a lift home, she said, and she still had that big old car. The passenger seat was ripped out, though, so I sat in the back with my legs comfortably stretched to the front. Wow, very roomy, I thought. Whatcha been up to, I called from the back. She gave a shoulder check. Not too much, she said and pulled away for good.

The trouble with writing non-fiction about sex in cars is that someone is eventually going to inquire of the silent air, was that me? Did he do that with someone else? Does he do that all the time? Or, considering the way that sex is usually conducted in automobiles, does he have that done to him all the time? I know that all my life I've had it hinted to me that automobiles are erotic places. Start with the car advertisements on television or in magazines. Two things: speed and sex. She's a fast one, fella. I am fond of the way in which a seat belt situates itself between your passenger's breasts. Or driver's. There are few sights so endearing but so quickly glimpsed and gone than a woman in a skirt getting into the driver's seat of a shiny car. Remember when we were teenagers or arrested adolescents – the couple in the back seat started making out first. At the drive-in movie it was a good idea to get popcorn because it came with paper napkins and you probably forgot to bring Kleenex. You know now that I am remembering all the places where I had my hands on the steering wheel and a lovely woman's head in my lap. Well, not all that many, and I am not going to tell you where, except who could stop himself from mentioning the Second Narrows Bridge?

*A*rt and traffic are tied up in my earliest academic efforts. Yes, I would eventually impress my grandfather's tractor into a tree, but this was just extracurricular tomfoolery in the vehicular arts. My two favourite activities in kindergarten were blocks and painting. My best friend Jason and I became more interested in the theatrical activities later in the academic year when we discovered the joy in playing house with the girls. It wasn't house that was the active part of our investigations so much as it was cross-dressing with the girls. At nap time Niki and Julie would stretch out slightly closer to us than they would to the other paste-eating boy-sprouts in our class. But blocks and painting remained Jason's and my first choice for an 'activity.' The blocks in the cupboard were large cardboard imitations of a dozen or so bricks in a nicely mortared cluster. Artsy Jason conjured a design which took precisely fourteen blocks. If you followed his steps you could build a very very cool imitation of a motorcycle seat and handlebars on a sturdy flat platform. We'd spend a good hour on these contraptions, making the requisite sputtering *pphplhblbhpblbhlbpps* while steering our choppers around the streets of Langley. Sometimes Niki or Julie might hop on the back of our bad boys and hang on tight around our stomachs like we'd seen on TV. Even better, there were only forty blocks to play with, so any paste-eating boy-sprout who tried to join us and build himself a righteous chopper was left with only twelve of the necessary fourteen blocks to do it. When we both moved to painting, Jason again triumphed in his five-year-old approximations of Snoopy on his doghouse. This made Jason even more popular, and his estimation by the class left me a remedial right-hand man, a wannabe toady in the gaga eyes of both Niki and Julie. I tried my best, but the painted images always fell apart, the watercolour usually mixed too thinly or the easel too steep. Fringes of runny black and red always raced for the bottom of my page. I must have tried to capture Snoopy for weeks. When Mrs Peggy McClay began her rounds to inspect the work, I'd quickly squiggle over my failure with another colour to bury my shame in a wild abstraction of criss-crossed activity. Eventually the question would come, And what are you painting today, Ryan? My considered response for several shameful weeks was, Roads, Mrs McClay, different roads. Pass the paste, boys.

Cars in my home town. When there was a parade there would be floats mounted on flatbed trucks, but there would also be a lot of cars with decorations on them going down Oliver's few blocks of main street, which was also Highway 97, and everyone pretty well knew all those cars. A few were antiques but the rest weren't exactly new, either. There were also decorated cars in a shorter parade after someone's wedding. People all dressed up would fill them, and the guy in a suit in the driver's seat would be blasting the horn. If the wedding cars went past us kids we would yell all together, 'You'll be sorrrrrry!' At the baseball park, before they put up the advertising boards for the outfield fence (which I thought got us a little closer to the big leagues), guys would park their cars in a big semicircle, facing home plate. Then kids like me and Willy would go from car to car, trying to sell Orange Crush and cool popcorn to the families in their automotive bleachers. All their windows were open because it was 95 degrees on a Sunday afternoon. Sometimes the PA announcer would ask the owner of the blue DeSoto to move it or put a blanket over the windshield because it was flashing in the hitters' eyes. If I didn't write these things down they would be lost from memory in no time, just like the songs Willy and I used to write. There was no drive-in movie or drive-in diner in Oliver, but they had both in Penticton. At the drive-in diner (it was called The Diner) just south of the high school and across the road, there was a big sign that said in vertically rectangular capital letters 'FOR SERVICE FLICK YOUR LIGHTS.' The L was so close to the I that it looked as if it said 'FUCK YOUR LIGHTS.' I never had the nerve to jump out and pretend to do so. But I hardly ever got to go to The Diner anyway. It was an old train car of some sort, a streetcar, maybe. Something exotic and bumpkinish. Something out of the US comics that we usually didn't get here in the Canadian Okanagan Valley.

*D*oing it in a car never got me in too much trouble but almost doing it before driving home did. I was seventeen and dating a terrific girl from a different high school. This made her mysterious, and made me mysterious in return. I imagined my classmates asking, What do they know about him over there that we don't? She was a model, too, like all girls in 1988. Most just happened to model for the same New Westminster agency. Didn't take long to figure out it was more a beauty school scam but I didn't blow the whistle for Jen since I could augment my mystery points with model-girlfriend points. Seventeen is the height of calculating. Jen gave me a string of her portfolio head shots which looked like those rows of photos you could buy from a booth in the Willowbrook Mall. The only difference between those photos and Jen's was that hers looked really really good. I kept the length of four wallet-size shots paper clipped to the sun visor in my infamous Acadian, much in the style of a young soldier overseas who would keep snaps of his gal taped to the inside lid of his foot locker. That was me, a brave man in the far-off jungles of another Langley high school fighting the good fight with just a picture of my heart's desire to remind me there was some goodness and beauty in the world beyond the wooden cheese plate I was sanding in shop class. Jen and I never did it but she was the first girl who ever let me put my hand up her sweater. Wow. That was when her mother pulled into the driveway. I wasn't supposed to be there, and neither was Jen's mother, so out the basement window I climbed with my shoes behind me. I lit for home in my car thrilled, terrified and, as high school boys used to say, blue-balled. I was trying to find a less uncomfortable position while I continued rewinding the tape deck to my favourite driving song. Jen smiled at me from the sun visor, all four of her. That's when I noticed what seemed to be a stop sign just passing me by as I shot human cannonball across a four-lane road at the comfy abandon of 60 km/h, or, as we like to say, clicks. A lot of horns and brakes went off around me but not one collision was heard. Nothing happened. I was the luckiest guy in town. I'd almost crashed two days into driving and almost done it just beforehand. Now the problem was I didn't know what to do next with Jen. The song I was looking for on the tape deck was the Smiths' 'How Soon Is Now.' Curious how much that shimmering guitar riff sounds something like a car horn whizzing by in a panic.

*W*hen I was in my late teens and early twenties I had lots of adventures on US 2. US 2 goes through Bemidji, Grand Forks, Minot, Havre and Shelby, where a lot of people used to turn right to get to Calgary. It was often an old concrete highway, and there were a lot of trucks beating on it in the fifties. So you might remember that I was once driving to BC with my roommate Fred Bing. Fred was quite a bit older than I. I think that he was in World War II, and he got to wear his bombardier's wing on his dress uniform, though he was just a photographer now. He had re-enlisted after trying photography on civvy street in Vancouver, I think. Anyway, it was the spring or summer of 1956, and we were driving west in Fred's pretty new Meteor. I don't know whether I really had a driver's licence or whether I just told Fred I had one. I had certainly not done any driving lately. But US 2 isn't all that hard – pretty straight road with no hills to speak of until Idaho, and mainly little prairie towns. So there I was, driving in my James Dean sunglasses, needing real prescription glasses, which I wouldn't get till I was 22 in New Westminster. One night I was driving in the dark and Fred was sleeping after driving all day, and I was getting used to the unusual trust he had in me. But sure enough – well, have you driven a prairie highway in the summer dark? – my eyelids drooped, I allowed them to close for just a second, to get them ready for more driving, you know how you explain it to yourself. The radio is playing late-night 1956 music, nothing more stirring than the Four Aces. Then all at once I hear someone shrieking: buh lop boppa lubop buh lop bam boom! And I look up and I'm on the left side of the road and there are two high truck headlights in front of me, and I nip over to my side of the highway, and Fred still isn't awake. Okay, our plan about driving and sleeping in shifts is not going any further. When I saw a crossroad I got off little US 2 onto a smaller side road, and then turned off that onto a dirt road, and then off that onto a road with high grass between the wheel-ruts, and then I got off that and turned off the car. All this in the complete prairie dark, remember. In the morning light Fred wondered how his Meteor was. Then he wondered where we were. We were in a farmer's hayfield. I had some time narrating what had occurred. It was a while before I could explain with pride that Little Richard saved my life.

Today's top ten songs about cars I wish I didn't know the words to:

'Drive My Car,' The Beatles
'Boys in the Bright White Sports Car,' Trooper
'Black Cars,' Gino Vannelli
'Maybelline,' Chuck Berry
'I Can't Drive 55,' Sammy Hagar
'Little Deuce Coupe,' The Beach Boys
'Pink Cadillac,' Bruce Springsteen or Aretha Franklin
'Low Rider,' War
'Mercury Blues,' Alan Jackson
'Get Outta my Dreams, Get Into My Car,' Billy Ocean

A—w, once I had to do a reading at Forest City Gallery in London. Well, that night there was a terrific ice storm. I was to be driven down to London from Toronto by Linda Davey in her sports car, and off we went. Once on the 401 we went into a spin, around and around, but still zooming along like a curling stone, and finally ended up with the nose in the median and the rear of the car up on the highway. There were huge rigs on their way to Detroit zoooooooming by in the dark with the ice flying in the air. I don't know how we got the car up on the road again and didn't get killed. We got to London late, of course, and got to the Forest City late, but the crowd was still there, maybe three quarters of an hour late; then someone brought me some hot Chinese food and I had to eat that before reading. I was reading the second half of *A Short Sad Book*, having read the first half there the previous year, and all on videotape; I don't know where that is, maybe at FCG. Then we drove to Greg Curnoe's place and Linda parked the car *on top of* a snowdrift in the driveway. Every tree in London had broken-off branches lying on the snow under it. Very pretty.

I came off just like a true young British Columbian in the early nineties because grunge music was from Seattle. Puget Sound fashion and Sub Pop rock were aesthetically low-fi and minimum wage in spirit. That suited me fine. Then, as a bonus track, Vancouver had the same rainforest weather, so we were already dressing the part to smell like teen spirit. Teen spirit, by the way, looks and smells like an Esso gas jockey. Our native look was all the rage. Coastal tree planters could proudly sport timber boots and it was A-OK if your pants hung loose and low with a hint of long john showing at the waist of your open flannel shirt. Never fewer than two t-shirts at a time under your Mack, of course. Those guys in, say, LA who jumped on the damp northwest haywagon of grunge must've been hot in their uniforms. Silly twits. Anyway, my buddies and I jumped into an old Chevy van and were off to a nightclub in our best Petro-Can duds, a case of Canadians under my feet and some heavy feedback coming from the dashboard. How BC, we thought, to be this way, three plaid-wearing long-hairs in a beat-up van. How Bob-and-Doug patriotic of us. Let's take a moment and pay attention to how perfect this is before it passes. And we did. Now it's ten years later and I have no hair and no flannel. I wouldn't drink Canadian with a ten-foot tongue and I often complain, I'll admit, that I don't understand the continued teen-angst fashion of wearing pants wide and low, as if you just shat in them and that's about as much as you think of this place. Then last week I was on my way to UBC to give a reading to a dozy audience of eight. My buddy in letters, Wayde Compton, offered me a lift, having recently renewed his licence and purchased a ride just so he could easily move his turntables around from gig to unsuspecting poetry gig. You can ask him anything you want about Black BC history on the way. But this was no ordinary lift. I stepped up into Proust's petite madeleine. There it was, back again, a beat-up van with no back seats and some heavy feedback coming from the dashboard speakers. We weren't wearing grunge any more, or listening to it; we weren't drinking Canadian any more, just local ales. We are older now, and more mature. Today we wear black for poetry and listen to Black Sabbath in our nostalgic vans.

*S*ometimes you are just lucky, and sometimes neat stuff happens all night. The scene is the old apartment of Laurie Jocelyn in a funky part of Montreal, the southeast, sort of St-Henri, sort of Olde Montreal, crooked streets, river not that far away, and it is starting to snow. But we are all inside, and you know this didn't happen all that often, but I had a nice supply of dope and had a good strong hit or two and gave the rest to the crowd. Then I apparently managed to fall asleep in a chair in the kitchen. When I woke up sometime later, you would hardly believe what I saw standing directly in front of me. The two most famous young women poets in the country! Both of them were short. Both of them started publishing in the magazines when they were teenagers. Both were famous for reading to the Chianti-bottle crowd at the Bohemian Embassy. Both had self-published little chapbooks of poems before they got famous. What a lovely way to wake up and say hello. I do not remember anything else from that party. But I remember leaving. There we were, Angela and I don't remember who else, all bundled and booted in the deep deep snow of the back lane where my maroon two-door Bel Air was parked. The snowflakes were huge and slow, just like movie snow, and my Bel Air was a white shape. So was the motorcycle policeman who was astride his machine, holding out his little notebook thing. He had snow piled high on his police hat. Now, I was going to begin by saying that I am the kind of boring driver who does not get tickets, but for some reason I accumulated a lot of parking tickets in Montreal. My friends told me that no one in Montreal is avid about paying their parking tickets, but I had gone to Station 10 and paid mine the day before, just to be able to relax. This motorcycle cop had been sitting there for a long time, waiting for me, because he had no way of knowing which building I was in. I see that you have a lot of parking tickets, he said in a friendly French accent. Well, it happens that I paid them off yesterday, I said. Of course, he said, and you have a receipt? I could tell that he did not believe me, and he was feeling good though snowed upon. Indeed, I do, I said, sweeping snow off the Bel Air's left door handle. I brought out the receipt and showed it to the friendly policeman. He took his time reading it, and then politely handed it back and gave me his thanks. The back tire of his motorcycle slipped from side to side as he disappeared down the crooked back lane in the falling snow.

*W*hen I was a student, the notion of composing with an ear and eye for open fields and forms didn't come quickly to me, a hopelessly suburban scribe with pretensions to open-mindedness. Had I been more observant than available to other people's influences I would have noticed, for instance, that I had a terrible time leaving in the middle of a good song when my friends shut off their cars. This is not the tendency of one who will one day write to 'resist closure,' as they say. When I drove through my teens, I would park and wait for a song to end, slowly gathering my crud bag and its bookish contents, stretching whatever minor attention I could give things – putting tapes back in cases, fixing hair, counting the cigarettes I had left for the day, dividing the day's hours by those cigarettes, scheduling cigarette breaks – until that sometimes very long song was over. But I'd wait. The drive must always resolve on a final note. To go from my parents' brown rancher in Langley to Kwantlen College in Surrey was almost exactly as long as 'Welcome to the Pleasuredome,' the Frankie Goes to Hollywood extended remix. Maybe it was a bit short, so I'd speed along the #10 highway to catch up with the song. And because of that academic-friendly timing, I often played this song in my car when I was late for early morning literature classes. In first year, we were always wanking on about characters and their motivations vis-à-vis other characters and their motivations. I learned that circumscribed cycle of influence was called 'psychological realism.' This didn't make a hell of a lot of sense to me. I wanted to know about the forms of things themselves. What do they do to us? No motivation but in things. Williams learned something like that from plums. I'm sorry I'm late, but I had to finish the tune first. It was so disco, so sweet.

*O*n my way up north Sunday, the wind caught my car on a patch of black ice, spun it into the oncoming lane, good, I thought, I'm going to miss that car and go into the ditch, good, no trees, lotsa snow, it'll be a soft landing, I wonder if I'll need a tow out, and next thing I knew, about six seconds later, I was upside down looking at dense snow out of all windows. Boots appeared in the window, I unbuckled my seat belt and the boots helped me out. Ross [on his way to hockey] and Michelle, his girlfriend [long red fingernails]. Ross's buddies came along and took him to hockey, I waited for the police in Ross's van with Michelle. Always eager to ask people about their work, 'What do you do, Michelle?' She said you don't want to know, I said I did want to know. Michelle's dream has been to be a funeral director, and when her mum was dying her mum said, go for it, Michelle. Michelle took her mum's advice, followed her dream, and now she's a funeral director. [It was a long wait because another car had flipped and the driver was trapped, so the police took care of him first]. I rented a car from the tow truck driver's girlfriend [he was getting a plane at 1:30 to go to the Super Bowl]. My car is a total write-off. I am fine, and sorta happy to be alive, I am exhausted from a week of teaching up there, & I'm exhilarated by the teaching, and now I gotta buy a new car. And, more important, figure out how to tell the kids and my mother without freaking them out, any advice?

xxx M.

p.s. Okay, I left out the part about the guy who stopped and wanted to take me into town to the Baptist Church [it was just before eleven on Sunday].
p.p.s. Forgot the smiling Baptist, and also the volunteer fireman who stopped and came back later and got into a big fight with the tow truck driver because the volunteer fireman also has a tow truck, though he wasn't driving it at the time.

I was going to tell you a story about a car but this page deserves no car because I've been too mouthy and proud. In fact, there are a number of cars and their stories not appearing on this page. Many, even. So I would like to dedicate this page to the growing number of cars I haven't written about, won't and never will. With them go parts of a biography, of course, little parts, long-winded and dithering parts. Regrettably, they had their chance and I blew it, blew it out the side of my big mouth. Many writers have noted that all the pleasure and impact of writing is easily siphoned away if you talk about it too much. You can easily talk the entirety of a book away. Those stories, as Gwen MacEwen once said of poems, become the gossip of the spheres, eternally bumping and spinning around the heavens with *I Love Lucy* reruns and the rest of the space debris. There they are, just hanging there, a cosmic mobile. Small, polished engine parts that still look usable, but which are unidentifiable for any function. I'm sure they're out there, so I'm looking up at them with apologies for opening my trap and letting them go that way.

*W*hen we crossed from Nogales, Sonora, to Nogales, Arizona, on August 8th, 1964, in our two-tone green Bel Air loaded to the ceiling with the Mexican stuff Angela bought, we didn't tell us Customs that the car now included a Mexican tire and tube we bought after our blow-out, and some Mexican wire holding the muffler up after a midnight repair in the dark in some stranger's yard high in the mountains above Guadalajara. And a big Mexican hairpin that had replaced a cotter pin that had once secured the connection between the gas pedal and the carburetor because the guy on the road to Puebla didn't have anything in the way of parts.

*W*hen I was sixteen, my friend Jasonn's stepfather had an obsession with the gas tank in his K-Car. Jasonn used to be Jason but changed his name when we started hanging around with another one – Jason One and Jason Two sounded stupid, so Jasonn figured it was better managed as a spelling issue. His stepfather, Terry, had bought a K-Car for his three teenaged boys to share. Terry's only rule was that the car could never have less than a half a tank of gas in it at any time. This was a funny rule to hear coming from his mouth. A cherrywood pipe always jutted out from Terry's teeth, so when he plucked it out you could see the little groove it had carved over the years. Keep it half full, he would order, becaussssse the dirty gassssss collectsssssss in the bottom of the tank and we don't want that sssssssssediment and crap running through the sssssysssssstem, boyssssss. The greatest thing about that K-Car was the effect it had on our enemies. A gang of shrubs used to hang out at Portage Park in Langley's low-cost housing zone. A shrub was a person who found musical satisfaction in such bands as W.A.S.P. and Helix. A shrub also commonly had long hair, feathered on top, wore a jean jacket and black and white baseball shirt with some band advertised all over it, and rode a chrome BMX bike everywhere. Our relationship with shrubs was awkward because we often bought pitiful bags of grass from them and, in that context, we were okay, but if they spotted us anywhere else at any other time, they usually chased our slow-running pointy-shoed asses down and beat the crap out of us. For me and the Jason(n)s, pipe-smoking Terry's K-Car was a cheap form of justice. On Friday or Saturday night, before going wherever we'd go, Jasonn and I would stop at Portage Park, cruising in with the engine and lights off. We'd watch shrubs screw around on their bikes in the shadowy park and, when we were ready to go, flick the headlights on with surprise and watch them scatter like roaches. The trick? The K-Car was the only car we knew that had, at that time in the eighties, the exact headlight shape of a Langley cop car. Ssssssso cold, sssssssso ssssssssweet.

*O*h no, said my little daughter, not another brown family car! All her life I have owned square-shaped imported four-door automobiles. Okay, I brought her home from the hospital in my two-door 1965 Bel Air. But soon after she was born I bought a square four-door Datsun. Then I had a four-door Honda. Then a four-door Toyota. Then a four-door Volvo, really square-shaped. This year I took the plunge and bought a dashing-looking car, but my friend Roy Miki made some crack I seem to have forgotten about a guy who will buy a second four-door Volvo. I drive boring cars. But more than that, I am a really boring driver. I cross over on the Burrard Street Bridge at the posted speed limit, 60 km/h, and cars are passing me on both sides. I always signal when I am going to change lanes. I even did this when I lived in Alberta. In Alberta they don't like to use turn signals or seat belts because they consider them to be limits on their personal liberty. I had seat belts put in my 1954 Bel Air when I got it in 1963, and when I drove to Mexico I kept the headlights on at all times. Whenever I was going to drive over the Hope-Princeton highway in the winter, I would get winter tires put on, have some chains in the trunk, carry some sand and blankets and candles, and get the car's brakes and everything checked. A really boring driver. I can often be heard making remarks about other drivers. The universal term for other drivers is 'asshole.' Sometimes, if I am alone in my car, I satisfy myself with hand movements and body language that can be seen from other cars. Not obscene gestures. Shrugs and hands raised, palm upwards, that sort of thing. I take other drivers at their word if they make no turn signal, even if they are at a T intersection. If I see a guy stopped by a cop who is writing out a ticket, I smile and lift one fist in triumph as I pass. In school zones I drive at 30 km/h at 4:55 even while the guy with his baseball cap on backward in the pickup truck behind me is a foot from my back bumper. I think the most boring movies ever made in the USA are those car-racing movies with Paul Newman or Elvis Presley in them. There must be some point to them, I figure, but I have never seen it. I have never been able to get past the first ten minutes of a car-racing movie about air force fighter planes called *Top Gun*.

*W*hen the press would come looking for old William Faulkner, the knock on the door would typically send him running to the back fields. Some reporters pushy for a story or a cranky quote would scurry after him, but sly old William Faulkner would go on pretending he was too busy ploughing the field and couldn't hear them over his tractor. I read somewhere that he would write on the bottom of an overturned wheelbarrow when pressed for space to work. I'm no Faulkner and the press would never come looking for me, but here comes my stop and it's all I can do to squeeze this bit on the back of my bus transf

*W*ell, I did eat the sushi at Koko's, and I remember how much fun it was feeding all the different radical things to Ryan the blind guy. I even ate the raw quail's egg. But I did not eat the little paper cup of seafood in salsa at the Veracruz waterfront. Willy ate it, and he had to get typhus needles in the ass at every city drugstore all the way back to Mexico City. There were ten of us drove down to Veracruz from Mexico City in two cars, Sergio's Renault and our Bel Air. Sergio and Meg and the kids Goyo and Sara-Dhyana and the just-born Ximena, and their dear live-in maid Elena, and Willy and Akiko and Angela and I. Sergio had to change a tire once, and some of us went to the symphony in Xalapa, but here is the moment I like so fondly to remember. After we had been driving south for some time, and it was for sure that we had fully turned and now we were headed east, I realized that Willy had been farther south than I because he was sitting on the right side of the car. Now, we were somewhat concerned about this: having studied in Osaka, Willy had been farther west than I, and having spent a summer in Europe, he had been farther east, because I didn't get to Istanbul until two years later. I did not get to Inuvik until ten years later, but I had been farther north (not counting air travel) because I had been to Fort St John in the fifties. But I could not let Willy get three of the four cardinal points. So I signalled to Sergio and pulled over to the side of the highway. I got out and stood outside Willy's door. Ah ha ha ha, I said. He knew what was up. He got out of the car and stood just south of me. I stepped past him. He went around me and stood at the edge of a corn field. I could see Angela explaining this pantomime to Akiko and Goyo. I ran into the corn field. He chose a row and raced south. Soon we were not bothering to stop in our chosen corn rows. We were huffing and puffing and the sun was directly above us. Okay okay okay, I said. Pues, entonces … he replied. We decided to settle the question in a gentlemanly manner. We stood beside one another, perhaps equal in southness. We also agreed that if indeed one of us were a centimetre further south than the other, we would declare this an official tie. Then we noticed that we were so far from the highway that we could not even hear the trucks go by. We could have heard wind in the dry corn leaves if the air had not been so hot and still.

*O*ne day my grandfather quietly pulled into our driveway, parked, climbed the stairs to the backdoor and knocked. Shave and a haircut – two bits. We wondered why the hell he chose the back door. Nobody ever went to the back door. Before opening it, Ma said, Hello, Norm, through the door's freshly cleaned window. I have some news, he said dourly. Oh no, she returned and unlatched the chain. No, it's the good news, he grinned. She opened the door. He took her hands in his. I've found the Lord, he said. An uncomfortable pause parked between them. Oh! she feigned surprise, not sure how to take this in through the door. He said, The lord came to me and entered my heart and is with me. Ma smiled pleasantly. Well, I guess I'll set an extra coffee cup on the table. Ma can be like that. Razor sharp. Shave and a hair-cut back at ya, big guy. When my grandparents discovered 'the truth,' they also discovered a cuddly affection for Rottweilers. To accommodate this new family of hounds they bought them-selves a nice baby-puke-coloured minivan. Good-news grand-parents in the front, bad-news beasts in the back. It always stank of wet dog and the benchseat upholstery took on more of a hair-shirt look. But the windows were really something out of this world: God's wrath manifest, the stinking rain of wormwood, the real fear made flesh-colour. Manna from heaven has its run-off, and I suspect it looks something like a half-decade of Rottie spit and snot and goop and guck collected on a minivan window. So, legend has it my brothers were in the back with our cousins, not exactly long-lost cousins, but very newly acquainted with us and our grandparents. The dogs were at home while my grandparents took my brothers and these cousins out to McDonald's. The kids in the back decided to play truth or dare. Now, I'm not sure what my brothers asked, but my cousins chose dare. I know it must've been nasty because my brother Mykol dared the cousins to lick a chunk of the window clean. He scraped a neat little square outline in the most bubbly and primordial yellow patch. No way! the cousins squealed. Okay, ten bucks, my brothers offered. Well, if you want to know how much ten bucks is worth to a twelve-year-old, it's enough that they did it, did it for ten bucks, and they licked that minivan porthole clean. My grandparents, too, took it for good clean fun. Our poor cousins. Welcome to the family van. Meet this side of your makers.

QUESTION: I recall seeing you read a few years ago for a PEN-related event, and was shocked that while someone was presenting material about the murder and persecution of writers around the world, a lot of people were chatting away. Do we take our political and creative freedoms for granted?

ANSWER: Sure, we do. Too many people have the same attitude toward human suffering other than their own that professors have about new poetry books. You do get more and more persuaded of this. Once when I was really young I thought that maybe one day if I set a good example, the majority of automobile drivers would start driving safely and courteously. No chance. I think that regarding human suffering around the world, things have changed. In the sixties it was a subject that was talked about among young people. I don't think it is any more. Now they talk about how they want a new car.

*M*ost car ads on TV sell their backdrop fictions more than good financing. Who wouldn't want an Integra railing 240 km/h along a winding and trafficless coastal road? Imagine, that air smells damp with pine needles and you haven't seen an insurance bill for days. Right. Ever driven the Sea to Sky Highway to Whistler? That's where most of those drivers think they are, on TV in that commercial, guiltless and free to burn dinosaur juice all along the toll-free highway and farting lemon-scented oxygen out the back of their eight-cylinder self-expression. But I've sat for four freezing hours just past Squamish while a tow truck or two essayed to unravel a cat's cradle of Integras owned by TV-literate leadfoots, about a dozen more with boom systems lined up in front of my ratty Civic, a dozen pulsing stubbed toes wanting to get on with the high-speed business of signifying. Where are they going, anyway? It's a question of rhetoric, I suspect. You know how madness is often outfitted in a rhetoric of place. Madness is somewhere you 'go' or 'went.' Sometimes it's a long wait on the highway and eventually we are driven there.

I went to the internet and looked up Phoenix radio stations, and it looks as if the time of soul stations is over just about everywhere. The one in Oakland is now some anti-intellectual religious station. I miss soul stations as I miss a lot of things there used to be in the popular so-called culture. I was trying to look up the Phoenix soul station because I have a little story to tell. I don't know, maybe fifteen or twenty years ago, whenever *Atlantic City* with Burt Lambaster was a new movie, I was on a government-funded reading tour of the US southwest and Mexico. It started in Dallas, where an ex-cheerleader kicked me in the shin, continued in New Mexico, where I tried to start writing *Kerrisdale Elegies* and played my only game of slo-pitch softball, and would later include driving a rental car in the hard rain down the poorly marked San Diego freeway and trying to avoid a guy in a pickup truck who was going to kill someone. Well, at one point I was in Scottsdale, and because it was Canada Day or Canada Week or something at the arts centre, they let me sit all alone in a theatre and watch *Atlantic City*, which was directed by a Frenchman but produced by Canadians. The next place I had to go was UCLA, but I wanted to drive to Tucson because that is one of my favourite places, and I love the way the desert starts to bloom about halfway down the 135-mile drive from Phoenix to Tucson. I have my rental car and am just peeing and washing up before heading south, and there is a black guy who is a janitor or something. I asked him the dial number of the local soul station, and he told me, so as I edged out on the desert I turned it on. You know those soul singers who once in a while let out a kind of yell or scream? Well, little Stevie Wonder used to do a good one. I guess he wasn't little any more by that time. So he had one song that just starts with one of those screams. Now, in case you don't get it, remember that Stevie Wonder is blind, and I know I shouldn't be doing any blind-guy humour, given Ryan's present and my future, but. So just before the DJ plays Stevie Wonder's opening scream, he says, 'Look out, Stevie, there's broken glass!' Scream. Well, you had to be there. I was so happy, driving along one of my favourite highways, in my favourite climate, far from anyone I knew, knowing that this barren landscape was going to change to a desert that just plain blooms.

*F*or a few regrettable years I sported shoulder-length hair and a short beard à la crunchy-granola tree planter. My family often commented favourably about how much I resembled my uncle Dave who has for decades worn his hair in a ponytail and kept a neatly cropped beard. His look is not à la anything in particular. It's just a post-hippie hair habit and a practical trucker's beard. Truckers, of course, like beards because the diesel fumes bite something awful at a freshly shaven face. Both my uncles, Dave and Allen, drove long-haul semi-trailers as long as I can remember, maybe even as long as Dave's hair. The occasion that springs to mind was about fifteen years ago when both my uncles were driving back to Langley from a trip to the Interior. They had driven their bearded faces into BC's semi-desert lands to do a little hunting. Although it was illegal, the only thing they bagged was a rattlesnake, and because it was illegal they coiled it up and stashed it in their large brown paper lunch bag. The theory was they'd bring it home, skin it, and wrap their dear mother's walking cane in the skin. The theory was that a nice snakeskin hobbler's stick would make her practical aluminum-walker friends take notice of her daring taste in physical aids. It was a good theory. Dave and Allen were driving home high up in the semi's cab, the freshly shot snake coiled in the lunch bag under Dave's feet. Somewhere near Manning Park they were stopped at a roadblock where park rangers were doing routine vehicle checks for any poaching going on. My uncles idled a few cars away from saying hello through the window while passenger Dave explained to his brother how there'd be no problem because most game won't fit in a lunch bag until it gets to the butcher. It was a good theory, but that's when the snake rattled under Dave's unsuspecting feet. Right out of a double-barrel those feet shot up past his practical beard and landed on the roof of the cab, and in the same motion his hands flew behind his head, snatched his .22 from behind the seat, aimed at the floor and unloaded his clip through the bag, snake and floorboards. Allen then commended his little brother for successfully shooting a snake in mid-rigor mortis, a snake that was stiffening up, causing its bony tail to wiggle and everyone else to spasm just a bit. The commotion was loud enough it pinned all eyes on my uncles and their laughing beards. That's why nobody happened to spot the old driverless Model A rolling quietly through my uncle Dave's semi story.

'*I* like the soul station one.

'I really think you should do a panel about your new car and how you keep it in the garage to protect it and then immediately scratched the side on the junk you are keeping for a garage sale. Now, THAT is funny.'

In 1982 my home town was undergoing its dispiriting transformation from a farming valley to a suburban fatty deposit beside the Trans-Canada artery. We weren't trying to hitch ourselves to Vancouver, nothing quite that ambitious. We wanted to be like Guildford! This means we simply wanted a bloated mall and plenty of parking. I think I wished that had come true when I was thirteen and learning to cruise the mall with my friends, ritually making goo-goo-eye contact with a cute girl, then looking back after passing to see if she was doing the same. If that happened, then you had 'eye contract,' as we coined it, which permitted you to talk it up on the next pass, probably in front of Bootlegger or Dee Jays Records. Kids like us, arrested in our pickup customs, filled the Guildford Mall promenades. We didn't buy anything, so there clearly wasn't enough of a market to support a sister mall in Langley. Worse, Langley got the booby prize. Because we couldn't support another boutique warehouse of epic scale, our dinky town played foster parent to a littering of ugly cousin plazas and mini-malls with 'No Loitering' signs. By their very nature, if you couldn't drive, you couldn't cruise the mall, either.

For a few memorable years I wore a bleach-blond brush cut and pencil-thin moustache à la Nazi Bugatti driver. My family never mentioned my look, but the couple next door looked askance at me because, they said, I bore an uncanny resemblance to their nephew Clyde, who dyed his hair white and had to wear a net over it while turning burgers at the Elite Cafe. Clyde and his little brother Mark had been working at the Elite as long as I could remember. The occasion that springs to mind now was about fifty years ago when both the brothers jumped into Clyde's Prefect and drove down to the Coast to do a little fishing. The only catch they made was a fully grown koi out of some gink's front yard pond in Kerrisdale. They stashed it in a big pickle jar full of pond water under a pile of fishing clothes on the floor in the back of the Prefect. The theory was that they would dig a hole in the front yard next door to our place, line it with concrete, and present Oliver's first koi pond to their aunt and uncle. Clyde and Mark were tooling that Prefect really slowly around the bends in the Hope-Princeton highway, and somewhere near the summit they were stopped by a roadblock where the park rangers were doing a routine check for fish poached out of the Skagit River. The burger brothers idled a couple cars away from saying hello, Ranger, and considered whether they had a problem here. Clyde explained to Mark that their koi did not look like anything that came out of the Skagit River. But, said Mark, I think I read somewhere that you are not allowed to import koi into the country, and two, if you did, you were supposed to have a paper from the government. We'd better make sure this fish is hidden, said Mark. But just as he was rummaging under the clothing pile in the back, it was time to pull ahead a car, and when they didn't, the car behind them banged into the Prefect, just as Mark was leaning into the back with his feet on the highway outside. The pile of clothing went all over Mark's head and the pickle jar slipped out of his hands and out of the car, and while it did not smash but simply rolled, the eighteen-inch koi fell out and was now flipping and flapping on the pavement. Luckily another driver had a full waterbag hanging in front of his car, and there was just enough to get the pickle jar half full. A park ranger was able to pick up the koi and drop it head first into the pickle jar. Drive on, he told the burger boys. Unluckily, the first night they got the koi swimming in the little pond next door, Willy's horrible dog Pal jumped in and pulled it out and ate the front half.

The casually observant eye can only register so many optical impulses per second. For instance: tire tire tire tire tire tire. You might see, at a certain speed of sporty car driving, six stations of the tire in motion. This would give you that blurry effect of a quickly rotating hubcap. With me so far? Now, let's say a ballad comes on and Joe Flattop slows down a bit. There is a moment when the six stations of the tire rotate at the exact speed your eye can process an image. This gives that briefest of illusions, the one where the car's wheels aren't rotating at all: tire. And, finally, let's say Joe Flattop skips his Alpine CD boom system ahead and cranks out a real thigh slapper. He pilots his machine ahead and our six stations of the tire break their illusory stasis. At a certain intensely zippy speed, the casually observant eye can only process less than a full rotation of the hubcap at a time. These images flip together through the optical sketchpad like this: tir eti ret ire tir eti. Yes, Joe Flattop's wheels are going forward, but the illusion has it the wheels are turning back. So where am I going with this, you ask? I propose we have observed the etymology of ecstasy from the sidewalk. It seems Christ embodied the many nails of velocity, then Zeno drove them home halfway at a time.

*H*ow soon after the end of the War did we start getting plastic stuff? It was fascinating, how they could make things out of this new stuff, even though you could see the line where the two halves were put together. It was also really neat later when they could put a swirl of a second colour into the first colour. Well, if you do not remember, you cannot imagine. I don't exactly remember whether Ronnie Carter's little cars and trucks were brightly coloured plastic or brightly painted metal. I think they were probably metal. We shot the shit out of them. There were two things I was not allowed to even think of in my house – motorcycles and rifles. My mother's family seemed to keep dying due to those things. But Ron Carter was like a USAmerican kid in a comic book – he had a Daisy Red Ryder BB gun. Boy, if my mother had only known. Ron Carter's dad was the town baker and also ran the Orchard Cafe, which also had a poolroom in the back, across the alley from the bakery. There was a long wooden gangplank that ran from the back alley into the upstairs of the Orchard Cafe, where I think the Carters must have lived. Now, this is a little hard to remember, but we fired from the gangplank at the little cars and trucks that were situated in a row somewhere, like the different birds you would knock off in that shooting gallery game you had when you were four. Those little metal cars and trucks, including a little tow truck, were so beautiful, remember? I especially liked the yellow. That's probably why my favourite colour became yellow, though it took some courage to say so. We would fire away at those little vehicles, and if they were plastic they would get blown apart, but if they were metal they would just get little dints or scraped paint. Red was pretty nice, too, especially on trucks.

One night in 1989 I drove my father's car to a stupid high school dance with Karen, my new red-headed girlfriend. The experience was the usual toxic combination of slow angst songs and clammy hands. But at seventeen this cheesy gym gala provided a night of profound almost-encounters with somebody else. When we left I turned my father's infamous car into the oncoming lane and sped down the road past the Christian Life Assembly where I would later have another almost-encounter in the backseat of another Karen's car. I didn't know I was night-blind yet, nor did Karen, so we drove silently toward the oncoming traffic. She must have figured I was showing off my daring at her expense and I figured I was driving very well, a mature straight handling of the car's poor alignment. Uh, Ryan? Yeah? Uh … What? Uh … Then two flicking highbeams realigned my reality and I yarded us back into place. As coolly as I could I wheeled us around the nose of an oncoming pickup onto the right side of the road. Of course it was a pickup, an almost-pickup. Karen and I didn't go together very long after that. It wasn't for lack of trying, though. I knew I had to say something when we were on the right side of the double-yellow line, something to save face or at least take the red out of hers. Now I suspect that's what bench seats were for. Instead of a complex explanation you could just put your arm around your passenger and give a comforting squeeze. My car had bucket recliners, so I hopped to it and coughed up a reason as best I could. I was just, uh, I was just trying to scare you, I said. When I looked across the emergency brake divide, I knew by the colour in her face there was no almost-encounter coming my way tonight. A repair, a quick-witted repair was needed. Wasn't that fun? I asked. Now I was double-yellow sure she thought they couldn't make a bench seat long enough for the two of us.

I used to complain when the cars were named after some ferocious animal or bird or fish. Or guns or something. All that USAmerican aggression. But then the Japanese and Koreans or someone took over naming cars. I get all confused after a while because the car will have about four names, like Levanta/Ciranta/Nellica/Topaza. If I could find a Barracuda I would buy it right now. So what the hell is an Impreza? I mean these are the people who started manufacturing clothes, especially shirts and jackets, with random English words on them: 'Rugby boy American fire fish elegant' or something. In England there is an English company doing the same thing, what the hell? I will tell you one thing: I am never going to drive or even sit in an Alero or an Altima. There is this thing called an Acura Legend. Now if that has something to do with accuracy, since when are legends interested in accuracy? Once I went to a leather-jacket store in some Vancouver suburb, because it was called Hollywood West. 'Isn't Hollywood already in the west?' I asked a big Asian-Canadian boy, who probably drove an Integra. 'It's just a name, man,' was his reply. This Legend, though. The word legend might have something to do with reading. Have you noticed that there are cars that bear on their rumps the chrome words 'Limited edition'? Edition? Okay, these cars have editors now? Is that why they have to be called Lexus? There is a German one called a Passat. Does that signify that it can pass at high speeds? Is that what this is all about? I mean, do those young people with their baseball caps on backward know what all these words signify? George Stanley's advice whenever you get annoyed with the car in front of you is: 'Ram him!' That's what I want to do when I am stuck behind something called a Lumina or an Escalade or a Denali, I am not making these up, or a Maxima. There is a girls' imitation sports car called a Miata. I am almost persuaded that that is an actual word in Japanese. I don't know. I am not going to get started on my other rant about the salesman's term 'pre-owned.' Doesn't that mean brand new, I usually ask them. Some of the US names on cars are as questionable as the Asian ones. Everyone knows what happened to the Nova in Mexico. And I have always wondered how many women are interested in buying a Probe.

*W*han that Honda with his financing soote
The bus pass of March maken useless to the roote
And dreyned every tank of swich licour
Of which pistons engendred and pedals to the flour;
Whan drivers eek with hir sweete exhaust
Inspired by every breeth and cough
Tendre ears, yet the younge crank a song
Hath in the boom system halve cours yronne,
And smale voices maken – uh – melodye
That cruise al the nyght with open window and ye
(To priketh pedestrians in hir corages)
Thanne longen folk to goon road rages.

*I*t was my first time in Europe, and I was doing it by car. It was the summer of 1966, my friend Tony was picking up his new Volkswagen, and for six weeks we would cover most everything between Sussex and Istanbul. We had a lot of adventures, and this could be a car panel about driving around Europe in a Beetle, but I just want to mention a day in Vienna. There were still a lot of Communists around Europe in those days, and it wasn't that long after the postwar events in Central and Eastern Europe, eh? Of course, given that Tony and I were young university profs, we had to be thinking about Graham Greene and *The Third Man* and that movie with the zither music in it. Now, I was pretty sure that Tony had been in Vienna before, and if not, some place a lot like it, or maybe it was just that he knew more than I did because he usually did, about anything important. I was just all caught up in the excitement of actually being on the European continent, as they say. Vienna for me meant wonderful thin wiener schnitzel, with perfect fried potatoes and lettuce salad with oil and vinegar on an oval plate that was perfect for wiener schnitzel. Tony showed me a rococo sculpture thing in the middle of a street and referred to it as a cross, and I didn't have a clue what he was talking about, but there was a cross inside this thing, I think. But the scene I want to mention is the Ferris wheel. This is the biggest, highest Ferris wheel in the world, by a long shot. It is very important in the movie of *The Third Man*. It is so large that instead of seats there are little cars with doors and roofs like those that go up the sides of snowy mountains. I will not go on those lifts and I will not go on a Ferris wheel, even an ordinary-sized one. So I kicked around in the amusement park while Tony went up to look out over most of Austria, I guess. I went over to the bumper-car place. I don't think I bought a ticket, because I was getting by on $6 a day. But I killed time by watching kids having fun. Then a half dozen nuns in complete 1966 nun outfits got into a half dozen bumper-cars and raised havoc. They yelled and banged into each other and anyone else who got in the way, and generally had a hell of a good time. This, I thought, was the sort of thing that ought to happen in a Graham Greene novel but never does.

Quand j'étais dix-huit years old, je suis allé avec deux friends pour la stereotypical backpack aventure neo-come-hippie. Nous êtes arrived en jolly France et, during notre premier nuit, were booted off le train à trois heures dans le morning. Zut alors! A wildcat strike. Despite it being late Juin, il était tres chilly outside, et chillier quand le breeze from le train qui départ sans nous blew across the empty platform. Il no rien jack squat pour nous to do till le matin, donc nous avons marched until we trouvons un terrific park de publique. It was un Vendredi nuit ou Saturday morning, depending how tu peut le look at it, et les flashy posters sur les arbres nous informons que ce weekend dans Nîmes boasts un grand festival avec l'art, les jeux, parades et, boy oh fils, a bullfight. Mais, il n'y a rien diddly à faire at three in the morn except assayez-vous dans le park et bottoms up le single bouteille de vin qui reste between le nous. About a demi-heure into les limited festivitees, deux étrangers nous approached and demanded – well, non, ils ont demandé – s'ils could en imbibe un peut de notre pitiful grape reserves. Non reserve ici, on a shared le tout. Then les deux on a demandent – non, they told us – come avec us to un party, maintenant. Nous sommes suspicious comme all get out, but nous sommes égale-ment chilly et desirous pour more bordeaux. On vont. J'ai asked whose party on va attender toute de suite et les deux hommes replied 'le big boss.' Ils ont whispered qu'ils just finished up un bon night's travail et must retourner to the place du boss, un restaurant Italienne très nearby. Qu'est-ce que tu fait? mon ami Jasonn questioned les deux. We had just marched to leur van, et les deux opened le back doors pour nous to load up ourselves into les avec. Le van était tout full avec les leather jackets, stereos et deux ou trois nouveaux tellys. Parce que j'étais so rigid frigid avec le cold et le nouvelle situation, if je could've je would've acheter un nouvelle leather jacket pour close to rien squat. It goes without dit, nous didn't want to allons avec les deux et leurs van-o-goodies pour le big boss, donc Jasonn a dit que nous couldn't, after all, on deuxième thought, aller au party parce que, uh, nous have to – comment est-ce qu'on dit? – waitons for someone ici, thanks all la même, fellas. Ils ne peut pas nous comprendées très hot mais je pense they caught notre drift about waiting pour notre man, si vous know quoi je mean.

*O*n the nameplate above the windshield in front of his steering wheel it said 'Eugene (Bomber) Lacey,' but no one called him Eugene. Even his wife called him Bomber. Usually we said 'The Bomber,' and when we were young we always wanted to be on his bus. Bomber Lacey drove the Penticton–Vancouver Greyhound run, and he was a legend on that line. Bomber never smiled at anyone the way Greyhound drivers are supposed to. This was because of the devil inside him that was chewing on his vital organs. You see, Bomber Lacey held the record for the Hope–Princeton, only he called it the Princeton–Hope. No one in a family car had ever made it from Princeton to Hope as fast as Bomber Lacey did it in a Blue Bird six-wheeler. If the damned thing was not going by so fast it would have been interesting to stand by the road and watch Bomber's bus go by, looking at the passengers from window to window, seeing the exhilarated college student followed by the terrified runaway wife followed by the old lady resigned to her fate. Bomber never went in for that Company horseshit about informing the passengers where they were. He never said a word on the highway. He was look-ing at a patch of hardened snow half a mile up the road. He did not hate the brake pedal but he had no better than a professional relationship with it. If there was a muffled scream behind him he never honoured it. The length of the road was his foe. He wanted to shave something off his record every trip. Once in a while we would whisper as loud as we could, 'Go, Bomber!' But I don't know whether he ever heard us. We were carsick well before the Sunday Summit. The Company probably had a policy about road speed in the switchbacks, but slow and steady never wins this race. For all the years that I was a university student on the coast, I rode back and forth to the Valley with Bomber Lacey. If Bomber was not back from vacation for another week I would miss a week of lectures. A lot of us thought it would be a matter of honour to die with Bomber Lacey in a stony gorge. But Bomber did not die on the road. He had a heart attack while shovelling snow off his roof in Princeton, where he and Moll and their son Eugene lived. Now when I take the bus to the coast I don't go in and get a sandwich at Princeton. I go around to the back of the bus station, to the gunnited little cliff. Bomber Lacey is in there. You have to look sharp to see his marker. It is black with silver letters: 'Eugene (Bomber) Lacey.'

I've never been interested in drive-by shopping or my consumer identity according to billboards, so the urban vistas speak increasingly less and less to me through my dirty passenger window. Often I have read writers who compare driving to writing, and that's an attractive metaphor, except I wonder how that metaphor carries my passenger's attention, especially through this city and its angry enclaves of gritty nuts-and-bolts writing about the real life of gritty writing about gritty nuts-and-bolts streets. I suppose if the driver is the writer, the one with her hands white-knuckling the wheel and a will to barrel here and there, the passenger must be the reader she's showing around the sights. I've never been that kind of reader, though, and I tend not to relax in writing when the driver doesn't encourage back-seat navigation or a little back-seat lovin'. This is why I think my gal Tracy's a marvellous driver. We've only had a couple of accidents, but they were perfectly respectable because none were on main streets. We agree that it is best to steer clear of those main roads, the Broadways and East Hastings, the Robsons and Fourth Avenues. Our desires as driver and passenger steal elsewhere, her enjoying the more frequent need for turns and the notable absence of congestion, me enjoying the block-by-block changes in rooftops, stray pets, garage sales, blossoms and potholes. On Main Street all we can do is start and stop, simply start and stop, only to see Burger King again and another essay at Esso. Then our car parts, and she's sandwiched between delivery vans while I'm pulling away, my attention sailing out the window into Toys 'R' Us. She starts and it stops. The Mr Lube says, 'Doing it right. Before your eyes,' but I want to do more than just watch. She stops and it starts. The city stretches before us repeating its grey and neon. I've been a passenger long enough to know I'm not interested in looking at our gritty life on the streets. Because, when you get down to it, that's actually how the writing goes on, in fits and spasms through the marketplace, and that kind of driving gives me the main drags.

There was no drive-in movie in Oliver. There was no drive-in restaurant, either, no place to flick your lights. In Penticton, along the motel strip there was a drive-in and then there was another one. There was one in Osoyoos eventually. I hardly ever went to a drive-in movie. Well, I didn't have a car, and most of the time I didn't have a driver's licence. In 1958 I went to a drive-in movie somewhere near Merritt with a friend and some girls we met. I don't remember much. I think I was pretty drunk. I think that was the night I came to with the bunkhouse stove all broken apart from the fight I had apparently had with big Jeremy Crowe the Englishman. I do remember, though, going to a drive-in movie theatre in the North Okanagan, probably in Vernon, maybe Kelowna. I was there with my best buddy Red Lane and his wife. Her name was Elaine May Lane. Red said she sounded liked something at a Chinese restaurant. Red liked to be dramatic in everything, whether taking the brown paper off a bottle of wine or frying sunny-side-up eggs. So here is what he did at the drive-in. For some reason we decided that Red would go to the refreshment stand and get stuff for all three of us. After a while alone with a good-looking Valley girl in an automobile at a drive-in, I saw Red approaching, his hands and arms barely able to contain three really big tubs of popcorn and three really big cups of Orange Crush. I just could not help myself. As Red was carefully accomplishing the last few steps to the car, just when he was right in front of the hood ornament, I gave the horn a push. Aw, I can see it now – popcorn and Orange Crush entered the sky like fireworks over a lagoon and Red was well up in the air, his four limbs stretched in four directions. I loved Red for the way he did that, and I always looked for a horn to honk.

*T*eenagers think as big as mobile homes in Langley. If your name is Bottoni, please don't read this. Ditto to you if a Bottoni named Marzia is familiar. I say this only because she was the entrepreneurial one who got us to a distant quarry party in Grade 11 by stealing her father's Winnebago. It was mega-comfortable riding in somebody's ample summer home to a winter party, everybody with a fat two-litre Rock-a-Berry cooler in one hand and no driver's licence in the other. Yeah, I know – stupid and dangerous. But flying around in the Rock-a-Bago with Marz at the wheel was no biggy at all. Returning it to the garage, now that was a little problem – a lot like George's problem with protecting his own car from his own garage sale. As Marz backed the wide ride into the narrow garage, we listened to something scratch a deep line clear along the side, headlight to bedroom window. I suppose you could say it was an underscore for over-achievement in vehicle boosting. But what was truly stupid and dangerous was Marzia in her father's kitchen the next morning explaining how she rode her bike into the garage last night and somehow dragged the tip of her handlebars along the length of her father's summer home. Later she told us she was grounded from any summer camping trips for about as long as that scratch.

I guess it was Sudbury I had come to by plane, and I always used to like going places and reading my poems and stories, and so why not Sudbury? I think it was Sudbury. Maybe North Bay. Or Sault Ste Marie. Let's say it was Sudbury. So there I am in Sudbury, and you always wonder whether the person sent to pick you up will recognize you. If you are Margaret Atwood they will recognize you. What you do if someone doesn't show up right away is look very busy waiting for your luggage, if you checked any. In Sudbury it was a tall skinny white-haired guy with spidery legs, and once again you thought about how a person has an entire life and friends and family and events that you don't know anything about and would not have imagined if you didn't meet him in an airport in Sudbury. Then I am in his car, and it is what you would expect, that kind of car. Anyway, it is not too long until he lets you know that he was a friend of your father. Now, this is always interesting, especially if it has not been long since your father died one March day in Vancouver. So what is the story? This man and my father were headed north for their first teaching jobs after university, to Terrace, BC. A year or so later I did a reading at Terrace, where George Stanley was teaching. Anyway, this guy, whose name I forgot easily, went with my father in my father's Star on the long rutted dirt roads north, carrying six spare tires, having figured the odds and the unlikelihood of service stations. Look at the map of British Columbia and see how far north Prince George is and then keep going, and remember that this bone-knocking drive took place in the late twenties, when paved roads were things that happened in New York and parts of Toronto. Then when they got, on some logging road, to the Skeena River, with Terrace on the other side, the only bridge was the CNR railroad bridge. So my dad and this skinny guy had to put the Star on the train for the last mile of its trip to Terrace. I know that it is impossible and stupid, but I really wish I had been there to see all this. And I am glad I went to Sudbury and heard this story.

I asked a vw stuffed with my friends, what are your favourite songs about cars? George had a daffy tantrum about car music, but it's amusing how many others named songs about driving, songs they love to drive to, songs about other modes of transportation ('the wheels on the bus go round and round, round and round … '), songs they like to sing in the car ('the wheels on the bus go round and round … '), and songs with a thin reference to owning a car in the first verse. Just look at them hamming it up like that. This is about as instructive as a MuchMusic camera in a crowd of Mississauga teens. HI MA!! THE HIP RULES, MAN!! I LOVE YOU SOOK-YIN – CALL ME!! I asked about cars and what do they do but wank on about themselves. Yet, in a way, the assumption here is a curious one: what exactly is a car without a driver or a passenger doing something to it, or in it, for that matter. A similar criticism has been offered about our English syntax. Subject wants a verb wants an object. Somebody's always gotta do something to something or someone. I LOVE YOU SOOK-YIN – CALL ME!! True, I've always subscribed to the theory that a bell is a cup until it is struck. But an empty car? Maybe just another auto without the mobile, I'd say to the empty, indifferent vw.

A—ll these years I have thought that Lionel's white 1965 Chevrolet station wagon was a driveaway car he was taking from Toronto or Montreal to the Coast, but a couple of days ago he told me, no, he bought that car, and somehow I was misled into thinking that that explained why the tires were so bald, and this only 1966. I can't keep any of this straight, because 1966 was the summer I rode around Europe in Tony's Volkswagen, and also the late summer we drove to London, Ontario, in my 1954 Chevy. Lionel phoned and I went up to the highway in Calgary and found him asleep in the car, pointed west. I keep thinking that we are supposed to be doing more than telling stories here, but I don't care how old-fashioned you think I am, I do like stories, even though I may not tell them right. Lionel had been in England that winter, and then in Trinidad with his wife Dolly. Now he was on his odd way to Vancouver, I don't know why. In New York he fell down the subway steps and broke his ring finger, which got all swollen so that there would be no question of getting his wedding ring off to ease the pain, and he figured that back in Port-of-Spain, Dolly must have been talking with an obeah man. Now here he was with this white wagon. Off we went westward but first southward, Sal and Dean, and no, how could it be 1966, maybe it was 1965. Anyway, we got picked up by the Mounties in Waterton Lake National Park for drinking beer in a public place. You could drink beer in your home, so I said what if this station wagon was a trailer? The cop said that would be all right. What if it was a mobile home? All right, I guess, said the cop. Well, we have sleeping bags in the back – doesn't that make it a kind of home? No, said the cop. He asked us our addresses. Port-of-Spain, said Lionel. This is why it was only George who went to court a while later. Well, we had a lot of adventures, including all the beer we drank in Nelson where we saw the priest that Lionel had hit up for money in the Toronto airport, and Lionel gave him his money back and I think that pissed him off some. But talk all you like about buddies on the road and all that stuff, here is the main thing Lionel taught me during that trip. You can heat a can of enchiladas on the manifold of a 1965 Chevrolet. I wonder whether Douglas Woolf knew that one? You have to know the number of kilometres or miles you can drive before your meal explodes. The hardest part is opening the can when it's really hot.

In my dreams last night, Stan Persky was driving me. No, not like that. We were just commuting to the local college where we teach, preparing, as we drove, for our morning classes, drinking coffee, gabbing and generally horsing around, as we do most mornings before we begin seminars. It was raining end-of-the-world-like and Powell Street teemed with more than the usual morning crunch. In my dream crammed in his Micra, Stan turned to me, a toothy Cheshire cat on his mushroom, and counselled me on the nature of beginning a book. 'Once you have the box,' he said, the smile colonizing most of his moon-face, 'and once you've found the voice inside that particular box, then all you need is a nice finish, a smooth conclusion to aim for. That's what I get off on! That nice smooth finish! You can fit just about anything you want inside when you've got that.' I'm glad I don't resolve myself to the interpretations of dreams. I prefer not knowing what the hell he was talking about, and by the end of this dream all that remained on his face was a set of smiling teeth and two eyes fighting to keep their rightful place outside his mouth. Despite the obvious, this must be a dream because Stan's books don't tend to have any sense of finish – whatever that is. That's what's so likeable. In fact, they don't tend to have a sense of beginning, either – no fanfare, no falling down the hole, no let there be and there was. To begin implies creation, but there only seems to be invention, what you do with the happenstance. We just wade in to meet him, river always running, see what he's caught with lately, dip in and out as pleases us. In my dream in his Micra, I don't remember if anything else quite as unbelievable as that speech happened. And in the end, I didn't get to find out what was going to happen with this story because the car leaned as we followed the curve in the road by Victoria Drive and I woke up. This happens to me in what some call 'real life' if I'm sleeping on the bus. I always wait for that bend in the road, awake or asleep, because that's how I know my bus stop is next and it's time to pull the cord and get off, or not.

*D*riving into or is it onto Gibraltar can be seen as pretty strange, but first of all you have to arrive at the border alive. If you are driving a little rented Opel, say, with two passengers and far too much luggage. You will soon understand why the annual surveys name the Greeks and the Spanish as the most dangerous drivers on European roads. You are driving along twisty mountain roads and occasionally you can admire the vineyards that fill the rolling landscape as far as the edge of the sky. But you do not look very often, and you seriously wish that the Spanish drivers did not, either. There is one with his front bumper about three feet from your rear bumper, and you have to drive fast with your front bumper about four feet from the rear bumper of the car in front of you, because if you do not, three cars will pass you and dive into the little space in front of you, just before they would have been loudly destroyed by a lot of cars coming fast in the opposite direction. You know that this will continue for every second of the next four hours of driving in these mountains. Now to those endless cars coming fast toward you. An alarming percentage of the time they are not on the other side of the road. Coming toward you and getting big fast is a car with a short space in front of it. Now another car pulls out to pass it, despite the fact that you are on that side of the road, and then just as you are thinking that he has a chance to make it before he hits you, and of course you are either on the edge of a cliff looking down or a cliff looking up, a third car pulls out to pass him. You wish that you were a Spanish Catholic, so that you could find meaning in your sacrifice and the sacrifice of your passengers. All right, suppose, against the most rational expectations, and against the odds probably offered by some betting shop in Madrid, you make it to the Gibraltar border. But here is why I said that this crossing could be thought of as strange. While you are looking up ahead at the road that goes on a steep angle to the top of the Rock you are waiting on the very flat approach to the British colony or whatever it is. It is flat because it is a short runway used by the Boeing 737s that fly in from England, bringing the daily papers and so on. The road you are driving goes right across the runway. With so many British people looking at so many schedules and so on, this driving across a landing strip will be the safest driving you have done all day.

*H*ere's another way to look at rhyme. I saw part of me go to hell through the windshield of my first car, that infamous 1982 Pontiac Acadian. The year is 1990 and I'm 18, behind the wheel of a car named for an ejected people on the opposite coast. A careful driver, I stop for the amber and enjoy being first for the next green, first out of the red. Hell, I think, I'm not in any hurry, so I stop for the amber and look at the red. My eyes glance just to the side of the lights. The red disappears. No green there, no red there – just, no. Then my eyes, curious, move a little more to the right. Poof, red's there, just off to the side of the visual field. Hell, it came back. Where did it go? How'd it come back? Maybe it's one of those bizarre biological paradoxes, I thought, something like you can't look at yourself looking. That's why Eurydice was sucked back down, right? The arrogance of Orpheus's peek-a-boo tease. I've also heard images can fall into the optic nerve, that spot where it attaches itself to the retina. 'Optic nerve'? I look a little further to the right. The red goes, again. A little further and back it comes, predictable as rhyme. Oh my god, there's a loud quatrain in my eyes. Off I sped to the doctor the next day, careful cars didn't disappear and return in front of me. Seeing is not a matter of mechanics but metamorphosis, so it appears. My parents gave me the Acadian I drove to my doctor's office. It was my father's car and when he bought a new one he kept the old one in the driveway for about a year. Yup, yup, yup, gonna fix it up and sell it, he'd say, but secretly he cleaned it up for my graduation present. To drive the old man's car and call it my own felt good and familiar, even if it was a blue Acadian with a hole growing in the floorboards right there under my seat. It matched what would be the first hole in my retina from a disease you can find a version of most commonly in the Louisiana bayous. The Acadians had it in them, then generations concentrated the gene's prominence and passed it on down to their children and grandchildren. Inherited blindness in the Acadian. There it is again, rhyme, illuminating the dark discord in things. If you ever go down, way down to the bayous, you'll see thousands of watery intersections to travel. Custom has it you always pay your river pilot in advance.

*I*t was all Fred Wah's fault. I had been to New Zealand or Australia a number of times, so why did I listen to him? Talking about the long long Boeing 747 ride to the Antipodes, and the fact that I was going to have to drive a car for hours and hours when we got there, Fred said I should take a sleeping pill and groove my way over the south Pacific. But why didn't he say that I should not have alcohol with a sleeping pill, especially at 39,000 feet? I guess I had a drink on the way to Honolulu, and some wine with dinner after takeoff from there, and then an after-dinner liqueur, and maybe a beer. In all these years that I have told people about that flight, they have always said oh no, you don't ever mix sleeping pills and alcohol. Now, I have always liked the breakfast you get a couple of hours before landing at Auckland or Cairns, nice fresh tropical fruit and coffee and so on. But this time I was deprived of my joy. For the first time in my life I puked into one of those airline barf bags. Then I filled up Angela's bag. Then I took the one that properly belonged to the stranger to my left. When we got onto the ground at Auckland for our stopover of a few hours, I thought it would be a good idea to get a taxicab and show Angela a little of downtown Auckland. We shared a taxi with a couple of strangers, and travelled by that winding road quick into town. Soon after we entered the down-town area I puked out the window and along the side of the taxi. The strangers got out at the next corner. With unsteady legs, I walked around downtown Auckland with Angela, looking at stores and the like. Then we got a cab back to the airport, where I had to walk really fast to find some dirt to puke on, and almost made it, sending a rainbow yawn across the flagstones in the bright sunlight. I got a couple minutes of dozing done on the three-hour flight to Sydney, but as soon as I got there I had my first New South Wales chunder, as they call it there, and stag-gered to the car rental. Now we met our friends, Brian and Robyn and the others, and split up into two cars and started driving north. After all this, it was not easy remembering to stay on the left side of the skinny highway, and then later we could not do that anyway, because there was a horrendous storm, and there were big gum trees lying across the road. Then it got dark. Right in the middle of Australian country-and-western-music country. I was so proud of myself, and so grateful, that I did not toss my cookies inside that rented car.

TO: Ryan Knighton
FROM: George Bowering
SUBJECT: car panel #46, I think

no, maybe that was #47 I just sent ya. Hey, am I
AHEAD of you? ah ha ha ha ha ha!~

—

George Bowering
Cannot untie knots.

TO: George Bowering
FROM: Ryan Knighton
SUBJECT: re: car panel #46, I think

It's a comin', it's a comin', just hold your
horses there cowboy.

Some patient driver YOU are. Oh, I drive slowly
to set an example for other citizens.

In fact, stick a pair of quotation marks around
this exchange and there's my number 50 and it's
all your fault. I'm finished first. O, the glory,
the sweet taste of victory! But who's counting.
Ah ha ha ha ha! — 'Ram him!', remember? That's
the spirit. What a drag, eh? Er — race, that is.

—

Ryan Knighton
Respects his elders

The main street of Oliver never did amount to much. It didn't even have a real name, as far as I know. It was just where Highway 97 went through the middle of town for about three blocks. We called it 'Main Street,' but that was more a description than a name. None of our streets had names, but some of the roads out of town did. Fairview Road, or was that just an agreed-upon description, headed up to the old ghost town of Fairview. On that model, we had what people called Sawmill Road, and outside of town, every mile or so there was a road going east and/or west: Number Five Road came before Number Six Road. Someone once told me, I think, that the street in front of our house was Sixth Street, or maybe Sixth Ave. This may have been some designation they knew about down at the village hall. There weren't any street signs in Oliver, or Lawrence, as it has been called. So, getting back to 'Main Street.' I am going to mention one of the great moments of my life. Willy and I had been away to UBC and who knows where else, but now we were back in town. Willy had his little red Morris Minor convertible, and I think it was a Sunday, because we were driving down 'Main Street,' and there was hardly anyone there. At least half of the parking spaces were empty. I was sitting up on the top of the back of my seat, turning in either direction, waving to a crowd that existed in my imagination. Willy was driving without looking either right or left, under a big banner that crossed above us and existed only in our imagination. There was one person visible in the doorway of some store, some guy who was younger than we. He waved back and shouted, 'Welcome home, George!'

I got it one piece at a time
and it didn't cost me a dime
you'll know it's me
when I come to your town.

It's a '49, '50, '51, '52, '53, '54, '55, '56, '57, '58, '59 automobile,
and it's a '60, '61, '62, '63, '64 …

– Johnny Cash

Acknowledgements

Some of Ryan's car panels have appeared in *dANDelion*, dooneyscafe.com and the anthology *side/lines: a poetics* (Insomniac Press, 2002). A handful were adapted as a digital-media project for Artspeak Gallery, in collaboration with Mykol Knighton, for the CD-ROM *Sifted: The Read Room*. The *Knight Rider* panel was adapted for CBC's *Definitely Not the Opera*. Thanks to Lorna Brown, Brian Fawcett, Mykol Knighton, Tracy Rawa and Nora Young for formal transformations and collaborative take-offs.

Some of George's car panels have appeared in *dANDelion*, dooneyscafe.com, and as *Above/Ground 152*.

About the Authors

Ryan Knighton is a Vancouver writer and new-media artist. He is the author of *Swing in the Hollow* (Anvil Press, 2001) and a past editor of *The Capilano Review*. He currently teaches literatures and other writing at Capilano College. When George spots a VW first, he continues to call 'Punchbuggy,' although Ryan continues to be blind.

George Bowering is a Vancouver writer. He is just finishing a history of Canada that will be published in 2003 by Viking, and recently edited a collection of contemporary Canadian short fiction called *And Other Stories* (Talonbooks, 2001). The game is called 'Punchbug,' and I am ashamed to have won it so often against my unsighted pals Ryan and Willy.

Typeset in Optima and Magneto and printed at Coach House Printing on bpNichol Lane, 2002.

Edited by Alana Wilcox
Cover photo by Mykol Knighton

To read the online version of this text and other titles from Coach House Books, visit:
www.chbooks.com

To add your name to our e-mail list, write:
mail@chbooks.com

Toll-free:
1 800 367 6360

Coach House Books
401 Huron Street (rear) on bpNichol Lane
Toronto, Ontario
M5S 2G5